CATLA
and
the
VIKINGS

MARY
ELIZABETH
NELSON

ORCA BOOK PUBLISHERS

Library and Archives Canada Cataloguing in Publication

Nelson, Mary, 1937-
Catla and the Vikings / Mary Elizabeth Nelson.

Issued also in electronic formats.
ISBN 978-1-4598-0057-1

I. Title.
PS8627.E575C38 2012   JC813'.6   C2011-907769-8

First published in the United States, 2012
Library of Congress Control Number: 2011943728

Summary: An Anglo-Saxon girl saves her village from Viking invaders—
and herself from an arranged marriage.

*Orca Book Publishers is dedicated to preserving the environment and has printed
this book on paper certified by the Forest Stewardship Council®.*

Orca Book Publishers gratefully acknowledges the support for its publishing
programs provided by the following agencies: the Government of Canada
through the Canada Book Fund and the Canada Council for the Arts,
and the Province of British Columbia through the BC Arts Council
and the Book Publishing Tax Credit.

Cover design by Teresa Bubela
Cover illustration by Juliana Kolesova
Author photo by Phil Walmsley, Forever Photography

ORCA BOOK PUBLISHERS
PO Box 5626, Stn. B
Victoria, BC Canada
V8R 6S4

ORCA BOOK PUBLISHERS
PO Box 468
Custer, WA USA
98240-0468

www.orcabook.com
Printed and bound in Canada.

15 14 13 12 • 4 3 2 1

*To the generations of spirited
women in my family who inspired Catla:
Rhoda, Dorothy, Laura and Clara.*

CHAPTER ONE

Invaded

Butterflies hovered around Catla as she sat in the shade of a late-flowering gorse bush. Tendrils of her long red hair clung to her skin. She lifted them off her neck, hoping for a cooling breeze. All morning she'd wandered on the headland above her village, scarcely glancing at the sea, where sunlight glinted on the waves. The fields were ripe for harvest, and she'd stroked the barley heads with their shiny beards. She'd watched a brood of young blackbirds, their black beaks open, demanding food. Autumn had arrived with the appearance of blue-faced asters and birds flocking for their departure south. She'd carefully tugged out some viola roots and added them to the late-blooming wormwood, yarrow and bits of lichen in the pouch that hung from her belt. Rebecca, the village healer, would be glad of the supplies. On most days these pastimes pleased Catla, but this morning her thoughts were far from her tasks. She struggled with the question her father, Athelstan, had asked again that morning as she cast her sleeping robes aside.

"Have you decided?"

His words played over and over in her mind. Olav, the peddler from York, had asked Arknell, steward to their lord, the Earl of Northumbria, if he could marry her. Arknell had agreed to the betrothal and had granted her two moon cycles to think on it. This privilege was not given to everyone, but her parents had forged friendships with both Arknell and the Earl during battles fought together over the years. Now, her time was up. This morning her father had said to her, "I'll decide for you and make the announcement at this night's council fire unless you give me good reason against it." Then he added, "Some girls younger than you are already wed. He wants to marry you, Catla." He looked at her mother and said, "Sarah, you'll stand with me."

Father's face had been stern, and Mother, who always held that a bride should be willing, had turned aside when Catla sought her eyes. Yet last year when Lioba had married, Mother had said that thirteen was too young. That was before Olav. Father's words chilled her even with the sun warm on her back. Olav had been welcomed as a friend. Already, some of the people in the village regarded her as betrothed. She knew the rest of the village counted her lucky to have a successful peddler seeking her hand. But her heart was not convinced. And she was just thirteen.

"You've a dowry, unlike other girls," her father had said, "but I think Olav desires you beyond that. He's a good man. His business is growing because he trades well and fairly. He has taken time from his business in York to stay a few days so you can know him better. You should feel grateful. He likes our village of Covehithe, and he likes you. It might be a long time before someone so suitable comes this way again. Think carefully, my girl."

Why wouldn't he like Covehithe? Catla wondered. It was beautiful and enjoyed a flourishing trade with the countries across the water. It would suit Olav well. Athelstan was a good headman, and people prospered here. She loved her village and the headland beyond it. She did not want to marry, not yet, and especially not Olav. He'd make her leave home and move to York. Last spring it had taken her family a day and a half to travel to York's fair to sell her mother's weaving. It was a rough, dirty place where slops were flung into the street. She'd returned home with the stench on her clothes and in her hair.

Norsemen who wanted land and a peaceful life as farmers, merchants and craftsmen had been settled close to and within York's old Roman walls for generations. But there were also runaway slaves and other rough men seeking their fortunes in Northumbria, the farthest northern realm of England. King Harold's own brother, Tostig, had welcomed many such men into his army. Father called all these marauders and looters *Vikings*, whether they were Norse, Danes or Swedes.

A few days ago Tostig had been killed in a battle at Stamford Bridge, just outside York. The few invaders that had been left alive had taken their injured and sailed home. Who'd want to move to York now?

"What will I say to Father?" She shouted her frustration and startled the butterflies. They flitted away, then rested on some yarrow going to seed. If only she liked Olav better. He said he longed for her and that she was beautiful, especially her blue-green eyes. No one had ever said that before, and she liked the way it made her feel. But he was old, his hair already gray. And he was bossy. He'd told her he would hold the family purse because she was not used to coins, that he'd make all those decisions. He'd hardly listened when she told him she'd helped Mother with her coins at the fair.

That did not bode well in her mind. And another thing: he stank.

"You'll be able to persuade him to wash once you are married," her mother had said. "You'll be taking care of his clothes."

Catla was not convinced.

"I'll not be doing that," Olav had informed her bluntly when she suggested he use a frayed end of a willow twig to clean his teeth and sweeten his breath. Would he take notice of any of her ideas?

Other people in her village listened to her, even though she was young. In the spring, Rebecca had taken Catla on as an apprentice. Already Catla was making suggestions for healing. She had added horse-radish to the poultice for Martha's twisted knee, and it had helped. Being discounted by Olav seemed a poor beginning to a life together, but Father John advised her to obey her parents' wishes, and she did yearn to please them.

With a start, Catla noticed that the shadow of the gorse bush she sat beside had shrunk to almost nothing and was edging its way toward the other side of the clump. She was late! There were fewer demands on her time just before harvest; it was too early to start preserving vegetables and meats for the winter. She had the usual chores of stirring the dye pot, carding wool and spinning. But Mother insisted Catla help prepare food for the short-shadow meal, the main meal of the day. Her mother was right—Catla's head often was in the clouds. She had better hurry, but she still hadn't decided what to say to Father. Catla scrambled to her feet. Her shadow slanted away from the village. She was usually home by now.

Then she saw the smoke.

It billowed into a high gray pillar from behind the hill where the cottages sat on the benchland above the sea cliffs. Fires under cooking pots made much less smoke.

What was burning? There had been no talk of replacing the roof thatch or the floor-covering rushes. The grain was not yet harvested, so it wouldn't be the stalks. Smoke eddied and swirled. Her heart pounding, Catla ran along the sheep and goat trails. Father John had taught her to make the sign of the cross when afraid, and she wondered which gods were listening as her fingers flew across her body.

She picked up the skirts of her shift to run faster, her feet scuffling over loose stones, the drinking horn and pouch bouncing against her side. The smoke soared, thicker now. Nearly at the crest, she stopped, afraid to look. Then she heard a woman scream. Catla's legs buckled and she sat with a thump. Who had screamed? What was happening? There were more voices and shouting. Some words sounded like Norse, but she couldn't understand them.

Even at this distance, the smoke made her cough and sputter as some of it curled over the hilltop. *Care. Take care,* she cautioned herself. She flopped onto her belly and squirmed uphill on elbows and knees, following an instinct to remain hidden. Small stones and sticks dug into the tender skin on her forearms, but she hardly noticed. She kept low to the ground because the sun behind her would put her in plain view if she stood. At the brink of the hill, she shifted forward and peered down into the village.

Smoke eddied and surged around the cottages. Then she saw flames and more smoke. Fire licked the walls and ate its way into the thatched roofs. Smoke poured from cooking holes, curled around the edges of the roof thatch and swirled into spaces between cottages. There were cries of terror and pain and harsh words shouted in Norse. Terror tore through Catla's limbs, making them quiver. The smoke twisted, and she saw men in black tunics. Vikings. This was a Viking raid. *Nord-devils.* She pressed her fists against her mouth to stop the scream.

The smoke cleared briefly, and she saw the invaders prodding the huddled villagers with swords and axes, moving them toward the other end of the village.

Her end. Where her cottage stood. *Nord-devils burning my village!* The smoke eddied. Someone wore a green shawl. Was it their neighbor, Martha? There was a tall man with red hair. Her father? A small child clung to a woman's leg. Was that her mother and little sister, Bega?

Her eyes strained past the village to the cove below the sea cliffs. A red-and-white-striped sail fluttered in the breeze over a long ship—a Viking warship. It was much longer than the merchant ships she was used to seeing in her cove. Oars poked from holes along its sides. The prow was hidden from sight below the cliffs. A figure of a sea monster ended the long curve at its stern, reaching half as high as the mast. Were its eyes searching for her? She ducked her head even though she was sure the smoke hid her.

But she had to watch. Dogs circled, snarling and barking. Glints of metal flashed. One sharp yelp cut off. A dead weight hurtled from a sword tip. Stoutheart? Her chest tightened.

More sounds carried but no clear words. The breeze shifted and though her eyes streamed from smoke and shock, she kept watching. Where was her family? She tried counting people, moving her fingers one by one as her eyes darted from group to group. It was hopeless. Whirls of smoke obscured the village.

"Oh ye gods, help them," she whispered. Was anyone inside the cottages? Maybe these Nord-devils did not kill as quickly as she had heard.

Two small figures about the size of her young brothers, Cuthbert and Dunstan, darted after a few pigs. Guarding next winter's food in the midst of all this? Her brothers might do that. A dog snapped at the invaders. Was that Bentleg, their brown one with the curly tail?

"Don't kill them, leave them alone, don't kill them!" Catla found herself standing and shrieking. Horrified at herself, she clapped her hands over her mouth and dropped below the brim of the hill, her body quaking. Had she been heard? *Foolish girl. Are you to be killed too?*

She eased back for another view.

She would sneak down to help.

No, that was a poor idea. She'd be caught too.

What could she do? She must do something. What could she do alone?

Alone.

Maybe that was good. Alone.

The thought cut through her shock.

She could get help. The invaders might not know she was missing, even if someone had called her name. No one in the village knew where she was.

Aigber. Go to Aigber, beyond the standing stones, by the river. The village in the setting sun. Aigber.

Her father was a longtime fighting companion of Hugh, Aigber's headman. For years Aigber and Covehithe had celebrated the Longest Day at the standing stones. They'd all been together there three moon cycles ago. Her village had taken half a day to get there, and Aigber the same. She could be in Aigber in less than a day, without babies, children, dogs and carts of food and bedding to slow her down.

The thought of leaving her family now in such danger made her stomach twist. She hadn't paid attention on the way to the standing stones; she had never been all the way to Aigber. What if she couldn't find it? What if she got there and the Nord-devils had arrived first? She wrapped her arms around her middle and hugged her sides.

Squirming her way a little farther down the hill, she sat with her head in her hands, elbows propped on her knees, her body shaking. It was getting late. The sun was dropping lower in the sky. She had to make up her mind.

One thought skittered after the other. She had to get help. She was the only hope for her family, her village. A voice inside her head said, *You'll get lost. The Nord-devils will find you and take you away. Wolves will eat you as you cross the heath. The barrow ghosts will steal your mind. It will be dark.* In the midst of her anguish, she sensed her father's presence and the words he'd once said came back to her: "There will be times in your life when you are afraid, but a brave person does what has to be done in spite of fear. You, my daughter, have the makings of a brave person." She hadn't believed him, but maybe he'd seen something she didn't know was there. The words gave her courage. She would go.

She turned her back on the cries and the smoke. With the warm afternoon sun on her face, she turned, put one foot in front of her and felt the breeze cool her cheeks where the tears had run.

CHAPTER TWO

The Decision

As she moved farther from her village, Catla's resolve faltered. Should she check to make sure everyone was alive? Were the Nord-devils herding them into the goat pen? It had looked like that to her. Maybe the Nord-devils were slavers. *Oh, let that be true*. Then she recoiled. Slaves! But it was the better fate. They would be alive. Or would they? Would the Nord-devils take everyone, even little Bega and her brothers? What would they do to her mother and the other women and girls in the village? Resolutely, she stopped imagining more, but tears started to form again and she almost turned back. Her mind argued as her feet continued down the hill.

Alone, she could do nothing against the Nord-devils with their axes and swords. But if she stayed, she'd know what was happening. What if the villagers were killed or loaded onto ships before she returned? She'd never see them again. She gasped. Her little sister's face swam in front of her eyes. Catla's words, last evening, had not been kind. "Stay away from my things, Bega." Why hadn't she been even-tempered like her mother?

She'd turned her back on Bega's apology. Even the tears trickling down Bega's plump little cheeks hadn't softened Catla's heart. Bega hadn't meant to put another crack in the pot that held Catla's stone collection.

If she were home now…She shook her head at her foolishness and clenched her teeth in determination. Her steps lengthened as she continued down the slope she'd so recently run up.

She didn't see the mole's mound. Her foot caught the loose dirt and she slid, then stumbled forward and skidded downhill. Twigs and rocks scratched her arms and legs, and a boulder gouged her thigh just above her knee. She thumped to a stop on her side. This time she didn't try to stop the sobs. Tears trickled into her ears and ran down her neck as she wailed. Finally she lay still. She opened her eyes but didn't focus on anything. Could she find a place she'd never seen? She was an herb and flower gatherer, a baby-bird counter.

Mother called her a dreamer. And if she did find Aigber, what if they didn't believe her? What if—?

She sat up and swore an oath, using words only the men in her village uttered. She caught her breath in uneven gulps.

"I have to do this. I am the only one who can. I have to." She chanted, "Have to, have to…" and wiggled her ankle to see if it hurt.

She stood to test it. A twinge of pain ran up the outside of her leg, but it held her weight.

She squared her shoulders. *I'm lucky. It could have been worse.* What was it her mother always said? *Knock on wood.* Catla bent down and rapped her knuckles against a stout branch blown from an ash tree—Odin's tree—for protection. She picked up the branch to help her walk, feeling a pang of guilt as she remembered Father John's teachings. She made the sign of the cross, just to be safe.

The sun was in her face as she started across the heath. As she walked, her mind filled with the scene she'd witnessed. The Nord-devils all wore the same black tunics. Likely, they all served the same lord. Father told her once that different armies wore different colors so they could find their friends on the battlefield.

But her thoughts were mostly with her family. They would be helping everyone, the way they always did.

"You're part of this family, and this family cares for everyone in the village." Her father repeated these words too often for Catla's liking. "My father did this, and so will we."

She'd tried to close her ears when her father told her to do something tedious or unpleasant, like picking bugs from the bedding robes. Or awful, like emptying Old Ingrid's slops from her cottage every morning into the communal pit. She still felt guilt at her relief when Old Ingrid had died.

"The lord granted my family this land many generations ago for our use, so long as we serve his needs," her father had said. "It was given for valor in battle. The villagers honor him as a just and godly man."

"But, Father, it's you who are the headman, not me." Catla had tried to argue when the sickness sped through their village last winter. "It's not fair. Ruth's my age. She gets to play while I wash cloths to mop up vomit." Now her heart ached as she thought of Ruth, her best friend. She had succumbed to the illness, not Catla.

The villagers paid their geld price to their lord, but they gave their trust and love to her mother and father for the fair leadership that allowed them to live as freemen. Catla thought about the helmets, swords and shields in the village, carefully wrapped in skins to keep the damp off the shiny metal. She wondered if the Nord-devils would find the hiding places.

She hoped God's ears were open when she promised that if she returned and found her family safe, she would never complain again about anything her parents asked her to do. Yes, she'd even marry Olav. She crossed herself again and closed her eyes to seal the bargain.

A sudden gust of love for her small village with its gardens, grain crops and small cottages stirred her. She loved the sea and the food it provided. Smoked fish and village-made wares were bartered at fairs in Scarborough and York for things they couldn't make themselves, like metal tools, salt and some of the colors for their famous dyes. If the people were taken, Covehithe would disappear. Her heart dropped.

She'd been so deep in thought, her fear had been pushed aside. It came back when she turned and saw the smoke, lifting high and dark in the afternoon sun. She'd traveled a good distance and felt a sudden hope and pride. Her family was brave. *I'm my father's daughter, and my mother's too*, she thought. Her mother was a warrior who'd fought alongside Catla's father and was famous for using the short stabbing sword and catapult. All the village women owned knives, but her mother's was beautifully crafted, a gift from the king.

It was hard to imagine her mother in the midst of a battle with a short sword in her hand. Her mother would never talk about it. "When you're older, Catla. You're too young to understand." But she'd promised to teach Catla to use one this autumn, after the harvest. Catla had used a catapult for a few years, and even Father had said she had a good eye. She put her hand into her pouch to make sure the coiled strings, leather rock-pocket and the few smooth rocks had not tumbled out when she'd fallen. Her fingers found the catapult alongside the plants she'd gathered. With a long deep sigh her mood shifted back to grim, and she ran again to flee her shadow.

A few villagers had asked her, "How do you dare to go up onto the heath with just your catapult and stave to keep you safe from wolves and wild things? You're brave, like your mother."

She felt safe on the heath. Besides, she wasn't like her mother, even though she yearned to be. Her mother was helpful, kind and even-tempered, most of the time. Catla longed to have hair like her mother's: brown and wavy, rather than red and tangled. Right now she wished she knew how to handle a short sword. What if someone threatened her? Suddenly she longed for an older person to appear and take this burden away. How could she, the dreamer, save her village? Her mother would know what to do. But she was not like her mother.

Nothing had ever threatened her on the heath. The wolves stayed away and no one said what the wild things were. She'd never seen a wild boar, although some hunting dogs had died after being gored last winter. Does and stags kept their distance because the men of the village hunted every creature. She didn't argue with her elders, but she wasn't convinced she was brave.

She wrapped her arms around her sides, gave herself a hug for encouragement and tried to ignore her hollow belly. She'd find berries. She'd find the standing stones and the path on the other side. She'd get to Aigber. The elders there knew her elders and her parents. Everyone knew about her father's father, a storyteller and wise leader. People would help when she told them about the Nord-devils.

Why have these Nord-devils come anyway? she wondered. The Northern traders were often at Covehithe, but they didn't have monster heads on their ships and they didn't come to wage war. They exchanged salt for goat's cheese, cloth and Mother's beer. They loved her beer. Catla remembered the last group and the way they'd pushed for more. "Move on!" they'd shouted at each other. "You've had enough. It's my turn, Erik!"

They'd laughed when her mother said, "I'll take my broom to the lot of you if you can't get along."

The men seemed to love it when her mother spoke to them like children.

Catla's gut twisted and burned, this time not with hunger but with hatred. The feeling was new and disturbing. *Love your enemies.* The words came unbidden, and she pushed them aside. Should she love men who burned her village? *No!* She felt no love for these enemies. It must mean enemies who hurt your feelings, not burned your village.

The sun slipped lower in the sky. Birds sang and hares bounded across the path. She caught sight of a fox's furry tail as it disappeared around a bushy feverfew going to seed. The calm of her beloved heath slowly lulled her fury, and her thoughts moved back to wondering why Covehithe had been attacked.

She knew that King Harold had won the battle at Stamford Bridge and that Northumbria was secure again. King Harold's brother, Tostig, who wanted the crown, had been killed, and no one mourned his passing. Olav had brought that news, and Catla had tried to understand it to please him. She wished she'd paid more attention. Maybe then she would understand why the Nord-devils had come to Covehithe.

With the sun sinking lower, she walked as quickly as her sore leg would let her, using her walking stick to support some of her weight. The leg throbbed, and when she stopped and lifted her shift, she saw an ugly bruise forming. Without Rebecca's daisy ointment, there was little she could do. She trudged on, hoping to reach the standing stones before dark. The stones would be a safer place to spend the night. Her mind skittered at the idea of a night alone out-of-doors. No one in her village ever wanted to do that. But the standing stones might give her some protection from the will-o'-the-wisps, goblins and ghosts the villagers feared. She'd dared to go up to the heath alone at night twice this summer. Now she reminded herself that nothing had bothered her except her fears.

She lined herself up with the sun so her shadow stayed in a straight line behind her. This was the direction of the standing stones, she was sure. She brushed her hands over her long brown skirt, the calluses on her palms snagging on its threads. Almost without thinking, as was her habit on the headland, she set her feet between the brambles and bracken, letting her body pick its own path. The setting sun should be in front, but in the morning it would rise behind her. Then she'd walk down her own shadow.

Aigber sat on the banks of the River Humber, but first were the standing stones. Her fingers remembered the feel of the stones. Every summer since she could crawl she'd explored them during the Longest

Day celebrations. She'd imagined their carvers from long ago and wondered why the stones were there. She knew from travelers' tales that there were other circles of standing stones elsewhere in England. They said that farther west and to the south, on a wide plain, a circle of huge stones stood higher than a man's head. The stones she knew and loved were shorter. Ancient, weathered old friends, she'd even given them secret names: Odin, Mars, Thor and Ravensclaw.

She liked to sit with her back against the stones, imagining their stories. Bits of lichen and moss clung in small nooks and hollows on their surfaces. Some stones in the ring stood high as her waist, while others rose a little higher. One long stone lay on its side inside the westerly arc, while another was set a little outside the circle to the east. She had often sat on the easterly stone, picking the small purple flowers that grew beside it while she watched the summer sun climb from its bed. The stones formed the back-drop to the tales the elders told around the fires in the evenings.

Once she passed the stones, she'd find a path to Aigber. She walked faster, and to keep her mind from skipping back to her smoke-filled village, she called out the names of the flowers she saw—feverfew, yarrow, bone knit.

But stop! That noise, to the right. A grunt. A boar? She stepped softly, then stopped to listen. Nothing now. No movement in the bracken or weeds. She moved slowly, her ears fully alert. It would soon be dark. As she pondered the night, dark thoughts came crashing in. Would she be safe? She longed for the noises of her family when they slept around her: Bega's wheezy sighs, Mother's whiffling nose sounds and Father's steady snuffling indrawn breaths.

Tonight she would be alone. Would there be wolves? Safe at home in her own sleeping robes, she liked their calls. Some howls sounded close while answers came from afar. When the moon was round as a coin, they would sing in chorus. Once or twice, out on the heath, there'd been glimpses of pointy ears amid the brambles, but she'd never seen eyes—evil eyes, some folks said. Those same folks told tales about goblins and fairies, said they lured men to their deaths, stole babies or exchanged them. Father John glowered when he heard these stories, for the Good Book did not allow for fairies. Still, many people did not leave their hearths after sunset except for the evenings around a communal fire. Most cottages had wormwood over the door to keep the goblins away. Now she was glad she had a stem or two and fumbled in her pouch until her fingers touched it, along with the sprigs of yarrow, known to turn evil aside.

Imagine trouble, it will find you. Catla felt comforted by her mother's words, so she repeated them aloud, in a singsong way, and pushed aside thoughts of Bega clinging to her mother's leg and her brothers protecting the pigs in the midst of smoke and shining swords and axes. The sun sank closer to earth, taking its warmth with it. The smoke behind grew distant. She was alone. The coming night seemed long and dangerous.

CHAPTER THREE

In the hills at Night

Catla stumbled over some twisted bracken lying across her path, regained her balance and flinched as pain shot up her hurt leg. It woke her from a kind of daze, and she glanced around in fright. Had she wandered off to one side? No, there was the path. She checked her shadow. It lay straight behind her. Her alarm eased, but she scolded herself. *I am a dreamer. I can't even keep my eyes on the path.*

Nothing looked familiar. She'd never traveled this far from home alone before. How much farther was it? Her hands clenched as her body straightened. She squared her shoulders, determined to stay alert. Her mother's voice teased her mind. *Watch it. Catla's got her chin out.* But thinking about her mother made her stomach wobble, and she gulped in some air to keep going. Her eyes prickled as new tears threatened, but she blinked them away.

The sky behind her was growing dark as evening set in. Shadows of trees and bushes lengthened. Gorse bushes blocked her view in front. She passed another one and stopped at the edge of a group of barrows, burial mounds of an ancient people.

Barrow ghosts. The words came unbidden, and she almost turned back. But where would she go? She swallowed hard. She hadn't wanted to come this way, but now she had no choice.

She stepped lightly to soothe any spirits of dead kings and warriors buried under the mounds of earth. The sunken paths around the mounds made it difficult to see ahead. Soon she was surrounded by graves. Her lips were dry and her tongue stuck to the top of her mouth. Had she already passed this one? Or that? By pushing her tongue around, she managed to create enough moisture to swallow, trying to loosen the knot in her throat. Slabs of stone protected the entrances to the vaults, but she had no desire to push them aside. Shafts of sunlight shone between some of the gravesites. At each sunny space she checked to make sure her shadow still fell behind her.

Stories about barrow ghosts flitted into her mind. Eustace, an older boy who loved to tease, had told her about them when she was much younger, his eyebrows arching and his fingers fluttering. "You'll see them if you go out the night before All Saints Day. They hide among the barrows. Don't ever go there. Gray and hungry, they are, with heads covered by helmets, but only hollows for eyes. Their long fingernails twist and turn. Their rags of clothing float on air. If they brush you, you lose a part of your soul." Her father had set him to extra plowing for his mischief, but the images were already lodged in Catla's mind. *Turn your mind to happy thoughts, like the Longest Day celebration.*

A sudden prickling of the hairs on the back of her neck and down her arms stopped her. She froze. She squeezed her eyes shut and whispered, "Oh, Lord of hallowed grounds, forgive this foolish maiden. I've stumbled into your domain. Safeguard me. Call back your ghosts. I must save my family. Allow me safe passage through your sacred grounds."

With eyes still clenched, she listened and heard a rhythmical grinding. Peering between her lashes she saw Agatha, her favorite ewe, chewing stalks of grain that jutted from her mouth. Catla's knees buckled in relief, and she came down hard on them. "Oh, Agatha, Agatha, how did you get so far from home? I'm very glad to see you. You bad girl, don't you know Dunstan has been looking for you?" She reached for the ewe to pull her close for some comfort, but Agatha sidled away, seeking another tuft. Catla chuckled shakily, picked up her walking stick and stood, brushing her skirt off and giving her sore leg a soothing rub. Thank the raven, no one had witnessed her bargaining with the spirit gods. Or talking to a sheep.

She moved more quickly and her stride evened out. She passed a smaller mound and wondered if children or women were buried here too. Then with a squeal of pain, she stopped. A gorse thorn had gone through the side of her shoe where the leather was softer. She bent to remove it and, when she stood, saw the open heath before her. With a few shakes to dislodge any ghosts, she hurried into the open.

She had made it past the barrow mounds.

The sun hung closer to the horizon. The shadows were longer and darker as evening fell. They hid badger hollows and mole burrows where she could twist her ankle again. She slowed her pace. It was dangerous traveling alone. No one knew where she was. No one would look for her.

Beyond a bush of goat's rue, its long seedpods almost at the bursting stage, a faint tinge of pink and orange tinted the low clouds along the western horizon.

But what was she seeing?

Alarm tightened her chest.

A pair of pointed ears stuck up straight into the evening sky, still and alert. Against the soft wash of color, the outline of dark ears showed clearly. "Wolf." She mouthed the word. Was it as intent on her as she on it? She stopped and peered across the bushes. It hadn't moved.

She needed to go on, but how? Throw a stick at it? No, it might attack. It must have seen her. She'd step aside to see if it turned when she moved.

She edged sideways off the path, keeping her gaze fastened on the ears. They did not shift. She waited a bit. Nothing moved.

Feeling bolder and a bit desperate, she moved farther off the path. It would have to turn now to keep her in sight.

The ears remained motionless.

She called a low owl's hoot. No reaction.

She sidled back onto the path and crept closer. Suddenly, the ears took on their real shape: a splintered stump with pronglike branches above the bushes.

She gasped and her knees trembled, but this time she stayed upright. She'd clasped her hands together, squeezing her fingers until they hurt. Now she shook them to move the blood again. She tried to smile at her fear but couldn't. The middle of her body felt like one huge ball of twisted yarn, as if Bega had pulled it apart in play.

She wanted to be home under her sleeping robes, not here in the almost dark with barrow ghosts and imaginary wolves. Her lower lip trembled. She felt small and alone, but her mind urged her along. "Hurry up, hurry up," she whispered. The sound of her voice encouraged her.

She skirted an elder bush and came to the top of a small rise. On a hill ahead, she saw the standing stones, half hidden by trees. The stones squatted to her left, their tops showing against a sky now shot with golden rays against a deeper purple. *At last. At last. Now, I'll be at Aigber before the short-shadow meal on the morrow.* Her feet fairly flew down the trail to the stones, and she smiled in giddy relief.

An owl called low and long into the dusk. It's lonely sound echoed the way she felt. It was almost dark, and there was no shelter for her tonight. Would she feel safer inside the circle of stones? Her heart bumped. *Why me?* Her mouth turned down. She hadn't asked to be here at night and she felt close to panic. Why did she have to be the rescuer? She'd almost rather be back with her family in the goat pen. Then she shook her head. What was she thinking? She was the one. Only she could to do what was needed.

Someplace in this circle of sanctuary she would find a place to sleep. Suddenly it was all she could do to get there. She felt an intense weariness and could hardly move her legs. Heading for the shortest way, she entered the circle by the side, not going past the entrance stone. Just beyond was the stand of oak trees that gave shelter from the northern winds.

Inside, it seemed darker. The stones blocked the low band of westerly light that had dimmed as the sun sank below the horizon. Where should she sleep? Her heart was pounding now, and she closed her mind to the dark furies that scuttled around the edges of her thoughts. There was Odin's stone. Yes, she'd be safe beside Odin, king of the Norse gods. It had always been her favorite stone, slightly to the left of the entrance. Its surface held many small dips to hold a treasured rock or small bunch of flowers. There was a small hollowed space at its base. She asked for protection and thought she heard a rumble of assent as she knelt and removed any small stones that might dig into her body during the night. When the space felt smooth, she squirmed down into it and looked up into the sky. Her belly rumbled, and she pushed it against her backbone, telling herself that tomorrow in Aigber there would be food. Was her family this hungry?

The black space overhead was filled with what looked like a mass of candles sputtering and flickering.

She remembered the night sky as one of the delights of the summer gatherings. This past summer she'd dared herself to creep out of the cottage and up her secret path through the bracken onto the heath. Her eyes had gazed in wonder at the stars. Some of them had tumbled into the sea and she wondered why they did that. Tonight she wanted to capture the feeling of peacefulness she'd had then.

But what was that? Her body stilled while her eyes shifted from the heavens to the ground. She lifted her head cautiously. Something rustled nearby. *A small creature, a little hedgehog maybe,* she told herself. Yet she moved as close to Odin's stone as she could, to feel something hard and secure at her back. She wondered how her mother had felt when she'd been a warrior and slept under the night sky. *If Mother could do it, I can too.* The thought gave her courage.

All went quiet. She felt in her pouch for the small piece of yarrow to protect her against evil. There were no little pixies, Mother said. No goblins or trolls. Catla could not focus. The stars seemed to jump around because tears brimmed in her eyes. She didn't want to cry, so she curled into a ball and tried to think calming thoughts. Try as she might, she could not stop the tears and she finally let them roll out of the corners of her eyes into her hair. What if all her family was killed?

Who would look after her? Not Olav. He'd be killed too, since he was in the village. Her tears rolled faster.

But my family isn't dead, she told herself firmly. Anger replaced self-pity. How dare those men come to her village and threaten her family like that? What gave them the right? Just because they had surprise on their side, didn't make it right. She knew if her father had been warned, he would have set the men with their shields for a fight and maybe the villagers would have stopped them.

She tried to picture the way this would have worked, but realized she knew next to nothing about battles. Why hadn't she paid more attention? Who was she to make this journey alone? *Well, who else was there? It had to be you.* A slightly sneering voice in her head talked back to her. She shook her shoulders to get rid of it. *What's the sense in listening to a voice like that?* Catla turned her mind away to block the dark thoughts.

What had her mother and father said to her when they were proud of her? It was hard to remember just now. She surprised herself with a yawn. She was worn out. Her mind wanted to rest. She closed her eyes and said another prayer, gripped the piece of yarrow in her fist and fell into a fitful sleep, crooning the little lullaby she sang to Bega when she couldn't settle.

Suddenly, she was awake, her body still. What had wakened her? Peering at the sky, she saw a soft orange glow toward Covehithe. It was before dawn. She raised her head slowly and looked around, then clamped her lips together to stop a scream. Sitting propped against Thor's stone was a man, his legs sprawled. He snorted in his sleep and his head bobbed. His hat slid lower over his face. She looked closer. Did she know him? What should she do? She started to creep away, but her arm tugged her back. Fighting a feeling of panic, she saw that she was tethered to him by a thin piece of leather. It formed a noose around her wrist and it led to the man's side. She crept a little closer to slacken the thong so she could loosen the knot. As she moved, she looked at him more closely, but with his hat so low she couldn't see who it was.

Her heart pounded and her fingers fumbled in her haste to get away. Where had he come from and why had he tied her to him? Was he a slaver? Her panic grew and made her clumsy. It was hard to see how the leather was tied in the dim light. She glanced at him frequently. He slept. The leather had been taut, but now it loosened as she worked the knot. Calming herself and steadying her fingers, she wiggled the leather carefully. She tried not to pant for fear he'd hear. He remained quiet. She was kneeling on loose stones, and the longer she knelt, the more pain she felt until she thought she'd have to scream. Holding the leather carefully, she wiggled her wrist and bunched her fingers together so that her hand slid loose. Once free, she rolled over and was about to stand when she heard, "Pretty clever, Catla. You did a good job. The only mistake you made was in getting a little too close to me. Your breathing woke me up."

Still flat on the ground, she lifted her upper body up and peered at him. She knew that voice. "Sven? Is that you?" It wasn't a stranger, or even a man. It was a boy from her village. Before he could answer, she rolled closer and punched him in the arm.

"Ouch! What's that for?" he said. "Oh, I suppose it scared you to be tied to me. I didn't want to wake you up last night, you were so sound asleep. But I didn't want you to leave without me. What are you doing out here anyway?"

Catla blinked hard. It really was Sven. He was an older boy—not one of her friends, really. He'd look at her sometimes and smile, and she liked that he noticed her, but they didn't talk much. Her father spoke well of him. Lately he'd avoided her and she wasn't sure why. Did he know Covehithe had been attacked? Suddenly she didn't want to tell him, to hear herself say it out loud.

"Didn't you see the smoke?"

He nodded. "Yes, I saw the smoke. Is Baldwin burning the old rushes? Cleaning up before winter?

I've been to York. I'm later than I planned. What about the smoke?"

"It wasn't Baldwin. It's Nord-devils." She watched his face change as she poured out the story: the smoke and flames, the ship in the harbor, the men and axes, and her decision to go for help. She spoke quickly, gasping for words, and when she was done she covered her face with her hands and shuddered. She felt as if her bones had turned to seaweed with nothing to do but wave in the tides.

"Ye gods." His voice caught. "Vikings. It can't be true! Are they Norse, like we've been seeing on the sea this autumn?" He turned to her and gripped her upper arms.

She wrestled her arms free and said, "Yes, I'm sure they're Norse. And it is true. I don't know about my family, or anyone, whether they're safe. It was hard to see. The smoke shifted. Even on top of the hill the smoke blew into my eyes. Too far to see clearly. I didn't see anyone hurt. Well, one dog was killed, I think. I didn't see your father, Sven." As she said this, she peered anxiously into his face.

"No, you wouldn't have. He's been in Scarborough the last few days. That's why I was in York, to see if he'd gone there after Scarborough was sacked by the Norse army, but I couldn't find him."

Catla's hands clasped each other in sudden alarm.

"He'll be all right," Sven said. "He's good at taking care of himself."

"They won't hurt slaves they plan to sell, will they?" she asked. Her body trembled as she spoke, but she tried to keep her voice level.

"No, they'll want to get a good price and they won't get it if someone is injured and can't work." After a moment he spoke, so softly Catla almost didn't hear him. "No one is going to turn my village-folk into slaves." Then he bit the knuckle of his forefinger as if to seal a vow. He was quiet for a little while before he said, "You're very brave, Catla. I couldn't have done any better." He sounded so solemn, like one of the elders.

Catla realized how little she knew of him as she watched his action. "I'm going to Aigber to get their help. Will you come with me?" she asked. "We can plan along the way."

"Yes," Sven said. "Let's go. We'll get a good start to the day."

The sun threw their shadows before them as they left the circle. Morning dew wet their feet, and the sky lightened from a rosy purple-red to mauve. Moving in front, Sven said, "I've traveled this way before and know the path. We'll move faster if you follow me." The sunrise filled the sky with glory. Catla was glad for Sven's company as her fear urged her on to Aigber.

CHAPTER FOUR

headlong into Trouble

Catla's stomach rumbled. "I'm as empty as the oat bag before harvest," she said as she watched Sven's back on the path in front of her. "I didn't eat last day. Did you?"

Her mind's eye replayed images of the invasion. The sight of the dog's small body flying from the end of the sword, the smoke and the shadows of people moving through it. She frowned and looked back toward Covehithe. A wispy column of smoke still rose in the air, but much of it had disappeared. *I have to stop thinking about the Nord-devils and my family. It's too awful.* She blinked hard and thought again about food.

Sven dropped back to walk beside her. He reached into the leather pouch swinging from his belt, took out a small piece of hard bread and gave it to her. "Oh, thanks," she said. "When we started walking, the ghosts were out of their graves. The cock will have crowed by now, so they'll be gone. They don't like the sun. Mother and I always say this, but Father laughs and says we must be light in our heads. We don't care. We say it anyway. Besides, I like to hear Father laugh. He's so stern most of the time." She stopped talking and looked at Sven. "When I talk, I feel better. Do you mind?"

"No, talk all you like. The ghosts won't care if we talk or not. I ate at York last day, and that's what's left. Eat slowly. It's not much."

Catla's mouth watered as she started to gnaw small bits from the chunk of bread. She glanced sideways at Sven. Was he teasing her about the ghosts? He was looking straight ahead, so she couldn't tell. She glanced up at his face in the morning light. Strong nose and jaw, heavy sandy-brown eyebrows, brown eyes and long ears that didn't stick out as far as her father's. A leather thong caught his brown hair at the nape of his neck. Over the winter it would grow long. Come summer, village men and boys cut their hair when the sheep and goats were shorn, with the same shears. It looked shaggy and strange until it grew a bit, but it was cooler in the heat.

The rising sun behind them pushed their shadows out in front, over the grasses and plants wet with early dew. A spider's web, spanning branches of the boxwood to the right of the path, sparkled with silver crystals as sunbeams lit it.

"We've got a good start," Sven said. "Are you afraid of ghosts?"

Catla glanced at him and lifted her shoulders in a little shrug. "Aren't you? Ghosts come out after sundown and follow people's voices." She turned her face away.

"I know many folks believe those tales, but I've spoken to Father John and he is not happy with that kind of talk," Sven said. "He told me so. He says once a good man, woman or child is buried, they stay in the ground, except for their souls, which go to heaven eventually."

Catla heard more than a hint of instruction in his words, and she turned on him, glaring. "Who do you think I am? Bega? I know it's not their bodies! Ghosts don't have bodies. They have, um, ghostliness. Father John might not know everything. What if they were bad people, like the men who are in our village right now? Do you think Father John would think they would stay under the earth or would their spirits go looking for human blood, or even human souls?"

"You're making me feel creepy."

"You started it."

"All right. Peace. We'll not argue. Let's plan. We should be in Aigber before their short-shadow meal. If the villagers come back with us right away, we can be back to the standing stones before nightfall. That is, if everything goes well and they agree to help us."

Catla gasped and her words sputtered. "Why wouldn't they help us? We'd help them. Of course they'll help us."

"Sorry, Catla. I don't want to fight. It's just that…"

"I'm not fighting! Why do you think they wouldn't help us?'

"They will if they can."

"If they can? Of course they can! There are plenty of people to help."

"Catla, what I am trying *not* to say is, what if they've been captured too?"

"Oh." Her stomach felt like it had been hit by a billy goat. When she'd had the same thought earlier, she'd pushed it aside, but now, coming from Sven, it sounded even worse.

Sven put his arm around her shoulders and pulled her to him in a quick squeeze. "Don't give up." Then he added, "That's just a friendly hug. Olav won't mind, will he?"

"He has nothing to say about it. Not yet."

"This one is for good measure." Sven squeezed her shoulders again.

Catla's cheeks grew warm. She liked Sven's arm across her shoulders. It comforted her and for a moment she felt safe, as her body leaned into his. She hadn't thought about him as a friend. He'd always just been one of the older boys. Old Ingrid would have said their fates were being spun together. The Norms, Fate's three goddesses, were creating her future as they walked. She hoped fervently it would be a good spinning, but she felt frightened and hollow when Sven echoed her own dark thoughts.

"So," he said, giving her a playful push away, "if they get organized to help us, we should be back to our village to rescue our people before the next sunup."

"I was hoping it would be like that," Catla said. "I know some of the way in the dark, close to home. Was there a moon last night? I didn't look for it."

"It rose while you slept. See, it's still there before us. Won't you worry, walking in the dark? What about those ghosts?"

"Oh, if we're together, I'll make sure you're in front. They'll get you. I'll slip away. Father John will rescue you, after I let him know." She smiled.

"It's good to laugh," he said, "but we need to stay alert for trouble."

Catla felt a spurt of anger. "I am alert. You didn't see what I saw. I don't moan about it every minute, but it's always with me, and I am alert. Maybe it's easier for you."

"Maybe it is. I hate what's happened. Now you're upset again. Look, why don't you tell me everything you saw?"

"You think that'll help?" She crossed her arms in front of her chest and flounced her head away from him. "It'll make it worse."

"Nay, Catla. Talking helps. A shared worry becomes smaller. You'll see."

Sven should know what she'd seen yesterday. It was his village too. But his comments had made her angry. "I've already told you. Do I have to tell it again?" she said.

"Not the part about you seeing the smoke and running up the hill, but could you tell me what you remember about the village?"

"Cottages were burning, and smoke covered everything. Dogs were barking, and there was a Norse warship in the harbor. Two boys, maybe my brothers, herded the pigs, and…"

"Hold on a bit, Catla. Slow down. Draw me a word picture. Can you remember how many cottages were actually in flames?"

Catla took in a slow deep breath to steady herself and uncrossed her arms. She thought harder about what she had seen. She told him again about the Nord-devils and their axes, cottages on fire and the way people were hidden and then revealed by the swirling smoke. "Do you think the Nord-devils will have killed anyone?"

"I don't know." Sven shook his head, looking sad.

"The Nord-devils pushed everyone toward the goat pen. It would make a good prison. They'd only need a few guards."

"I agree. How do you know the Vikings were Norsemen? Maybe they were Danes."

"They spoke Norse. I heard it but was too far away to hear what they said. I know a few words. Old Ingrid taught me a little Norse, and Father and Mother speak it some. Besides, the ship was a warship like those that sailed past the cove on their way to battle some days ago."

"All right. How many Norsemen were there?"

"I couldn't tell. I tried to count but I just don't know."

"Did it seem like a lot? More than our village?"

"Maybe so," Catla said. "There was one ship in our cove. I don't know how many men it takes to sail one of those. It was really long."

"Not many or quite a few, depending on how far they go. They'd plan on using captured slaves to work the oars. They'd get about thirty rowers from our village. They might be planning to raid other villages as well."

"Aigber." They said it at the same time.

"We need to hurry" said Catla, and they picked up their speed. "That's all I remember. I ducked down and then made myself look again, but there was even more smoke by that time, so I couldn't see any better. I was so scared, Sven. Still am."

They walked in silence for a while, and then Catla said, "I do feel a little lighter. Let's talk about something else now. Why do you know this path so well, Sven? You're not a smuggler, are you?"

"Smuggler? What gave you that idea?"

"I don't know. Olav talked to me about smuggling. He'd like to see it stopped."

"What do you think, Catla?'

Sven's question caught her by surprise. He wanted her opinion. And he looked interested.

"Do you use a willow twig on your teeth, Sven?" she asked.

He laughed. "Yes, but what has that got to do with smuggling?"

"Maybe nothing. Likely, nothing." But she smiled at him in return.

"Olav says smugglers expect real coins for pay," Catla said. "If people have coins, he says they shouldn't buy from smugglers."

"It's not always like that, but I agree in some ways," Sven said. "Some fellows I know in Aigber and York have talked about smuggling, but I've never done it. Only wondered how it's done. I've never been all the way to Aigber. My pals from Aigber have come to Covehithe many a time. My cottage was a good meeting place with Father gone so much. I got quite good at picking up the trails on this part of the heath."

"At Covehithe? I never saw them," Catla said. "When did they come?"

"After dark."

With that blunt statement, the discussion about smuggling seemed to be over, but Catla intended to ask more questions if they could ever think beyond Norsemen.

As the sun climbed higher in the sky, her footsteps dragged and her leg pounded with short jabs of pain. She'd forgotten her walking stick at the stone circle but didn't tell Sven about her injury for fear he might slow down. She dropped back and trudged after him, thinking of the dreadful stories she'd heard about the way captured women were treated. Her heart ached for her mother. What was happening back home? The elder bushes rose over her head and the path narrowed. She rounded a bend scarcely looking ahead and didn't see Sven's legs sprawled on the ground. She tripped and fell flat on top of him. A shock of pain ran the length of her leg. She pressed her lips together so she wouldn't yell.

"Sven, are you hurt?"

He snorted out a laugh and rolled her off. "No. I tripped into this little rill. It's so narrow and silent, I didn't see it or hear it. Have a drink. It's good. My beer has been gone for some time."

Catla flopped down and looked down into a shine of clear cool water almost hidden by long sedges on both sides. She put her mouth close to the water, scooped it up with both hands, drank and then filled her drinking horn. She doused her head and ran her wet hands over her neck and arms. She stayed bent over for an instant and caught a glimpse of herself. Her tangled hair was still red—funny that her eyebrows were darker. She stirred her image into ripples and sat up. Her skin tingled and her wet hair cooled her back.

As she wrung some of the water from it, she scanned the bushes across the brook. "Blackberries!" They shouted in unison and leaped across the rivulet. Soon their mouths were jammed full. The thorns, sturdy and sharp, drew blood and plucked at their skin and clothing if their hands were too eager. The berries were purple-black with juice and as round as the knob on the top of Catla's spindle at home. Occasionally a tart one puckered the insides of her mouth and her lips squeezed as tight as a purse string.

Purple juice dripped down Sven's lips and chin.

Catla grinned at him, knowing she looked the same. Her tongue shriveled with the sweet, tart taste. She felt less hollow. The morning sun was warm. "I feel better," she said. "Do you?"

Sven grinned, showing purple teeth, and nodded. They walked on with renewed energy.

When their shadows were about half the length they had been after their blackberry feast, Catla said, "Shouldn't we be there by now? Are we close?"

"I've never been this far, so I'm not sure where we are. Let's just keep going." Sven's tone was abrupt and distracted.

Catla felt the sting of his tone. She opened her mouth to tell him to keep his bad temper to himself, but said instead, "All right. You didn't tell me you were lost!" She kept her voice light even though she was annoyed. "You needn't growl at me. Maybe we should separate. I could go down closer toward the river and you could go farther inland, but toward the river too. We'll meet later." She'd show him she could make a plan, too, and look after herself. Did he think just because he was older that he was in charge?

"Oh, yes, that's a fine idea." Sarcasm dripped off his tongue. "Two of us alone up here and neither knowing where the other is or if we going in the same direction? What if there were more Norsemen? Oh yes, good idea."

"You didn't hear it all," Catla shouted, "and don't talk to me like that. It was a decent idea!"

Sven stopped walking. "By the goat's beard, Catla, I'm sorry. Mother used to say my bark was worse than a seal's. I'm not sure where we are, or how far we have to go. I don't think we're lost exactly, but we should stay together. I haven't been on this path before."

Relief washed over her. She hadn't wanted to go off alone. She felt safer with Sven. Had they missed Aigber? She thought they'd gone farther than she'd walked last day. As she peered around, her eyes lit on a high point on the heath.

"See the hill ahead, with the elder bushes on top? I'll go up and have a look around," Catla said. "Maybe I'll see Aigber."

"Good thinking. Let's go," Sven said.

Catla set off in the lead. After a few steps, her nose caught a slight whiff of smoke and she whirled back around to him. "I knew we were close. Smoke! I smell smoke, cooking smoke. It's the village. We're almost there. We must be close." She turned and started to run.

"Catla, stop! What are you running into?"

Her heart lurched while her feet skidded to a stop over some loose pebbles. His loud whisper sounded like a roar in her ears. The urgency in his voice scared her.

Sven walked up to her, his forehead furrowed. "Slow down and think." His lowered voice sounded serious. "We're in a dangerous situation. If we're caught, no one will help our people." Then more softly, he said, "I don't mean to snarl at you, but we can't afford a mistake."

Catla's cheeks burned at her recklessness. "Sorry, Sven. I'm anxious. I don't want to slow you down."

Sven nodded. "You're quick enough, Catla. I count on you. Do you still smell smoke?"

She nodded.

"I don't smell it, but I trust you do. Climb the hill, staying low to the ground behind the elders while you look around. I'll keep watch down here. Maybe it's Aigber. Smoke means people; let's find out who they are."

Catla turned and picked her way uphill. As she climbed, she scanned the land around. Close to the top she dropped to her hands and knees and then lay flat. She shifted forward under the cover of the bushes. Wisps of smoke rose in front of her into the still air.

Edging closer, she kept her head at ground level until she could see over the rise. Anticipation made her mouth dry. She gasped and dug her fingers into the earth in front of her. Nord-devils in a small group sat at a low flickering fire. New fears grated down her spine. *They'll see me, know I'm here. Keep low. Keep low.* A shiver ran under her ribs and quivered like she'd swallowed water from the winter snows. She might have run into them. She ducked her head and pushed her way back down to Sven. "Nord-devils," she whispered. Her face felt stone hard.

"How many?"

"Five. They've got swords and axes. Their leather helmets coming over their noses make it look like they don't have any eyes, like they're barrow ghosts or something. Their tunics are black, like the Nord-devils in our village. They must be from the same ship."

"What are they doing? Did you see a ship?"

"No. I didn't look. They're just sitting. No one moved. Come on, you have to see." She plucked at the sleeve of his shift and tugged him forward.

They crawled up the hill, Sven following close on Catla's heels. At the top they edged together and lifted their heads to look down to the fire. Catla shuddered to see the enemy so close. Images of her village—the smoke and the axes, the confusion and fear—returned.

The fire had died to a few embers. The men sat at ease, their swords and broadaxes near their hands. Catla saw the River Humber beyond them, but the water's edge was below the bank, out of her view. Sven dug his elbow into her arm and jerked his head. They wormed back downhill.

"Whew," Sven muttered at the bottom. "That could have been bad. You almost ran into them."

The knot in Catla's belly tightened. She clutched her middle and asked a quick blessing of Our Lady. At the same time, she knocked her knuckles against a piece of wood, to avert evil. She wanted protection from all sorts of gods. "What are they doing?" she whispered, her mouth next to Sven's ear. "I didn't see a ship. It must be on the river." Fear at her close brush with danger made her voice shake, and she sat down abruptly, wrapping her arms around her knees to stop them from trembling. She was as close to danger as she'd ever been, and her muscles would not stop twitching. She doubted her legs would hold her if she stood, so she shifted closer to where Sven crouched.

His lips almost brushed her ear when he spoke. "Drink some water. It will settle you. Were you thinking of home?"

Catla nodded and raised her drinking horn to her mouth. "They're so close."

"I think they're going to Aigber," Sven whispered back.

"Yes. We have to get there first," hissed Catla. "There must be more men and a ship. They wouldn't walk from Covehithe."

"No, they'll have a ship," Sven spoke in an under-tone. "They'll need it to hold the slaves. What will they do next? If they scout the heath, they'll see us, it's so open here. We're in a tricky situation. We'll have to go back up to hide."

"Behind the bushes." Catla nodded agreement. She stood to move, her legs almost giving way.

Careful not to disturb even one pebble, they crept back up the hill again. They watched as the men stood, spread the cooling ashes, gathered their swords and axes and looked around. Finally, they turned and gazed directly at the hill. Catla urged herself. *Be ready.* She lowered her head as Sven's eyes brushed hers.

The Nord-devils turned, walked to the river and stepped down a narrow cut in the bank's edge above the water. One by one, they disappeared. For a few long moments Catla dared not move for fear they would reappear. Then she quietly exhaled as Sven touched her shoulder. They crept back down the hill and moved cautiously to the edge of the riverbank, using small bushes as cover. From there they peered at the water.

A ship was easing into the current, headed upriver. "It's going the same direction we are, toward Aigber," Catla said in a whisper. "They look like the Nord-devils from Covehithe."

"Yes," Sven said. "We have to warn Aigber."

The path was well worn on the far side of the hill. They ran and ran. Catla felt desperate. If the people in

Aigber were captured or killed, no one would be saved, not here or in Covehithe. Eventually, she had a stitch in her side and she called to Sven, "I need to walk." He nodded and waited for her to catch up with him. As she slowed her pace her heart stopped its pounding. Then they topped a small rise.

"I see cottages. There's Aigber. Come on. I think we're in time." Catla pelted off, her spirits alive again and full of hope. She didn't wait to hear Sven's reply.

CHAPTER FIVE

The Village in the Setting Sun

Catla and Sven hurried along the dusty, narrow pathway between the cottages in Aigber. Her eyes pricked, it looked so familiar, so like home. No one called a greeting, and the village felt eerily quiet. Where was everyone? The path ended at a clearing beside the river cliff, sheltered by a single oak tree. Runes and carved figures scarred its bark. The canopy of leaves, some already brittle and brown, hung over hand-hewn wooden stools, benches and slabs of tree trunks—the place of council. A rusted metal hoop hung from a leather strap over one of the branches. Close by, Catla heard someone pounding stone on wood in the otherwise still air. A knot formed in her empty belly.

"You, you there!" The old man's voice was hard and loud. "What're you doing? Who are you? Where'd you come from? Take off, before I set the dogs on you!"

Catla's voice wobbled at this harsh greeting. "We need help."

"Vikings! Norsemen!" Sven shouted. "Covehithe is burning."

"Nord-devils! Nord-devils are coming on the river!" Catla cried. "Call a council. Call everyone!"

The man scowled. "Call a council? Who do you think you are? I've a good mind—" He raised his stick over his head.

"Wulfric, wait! Father."

Catla turned and saw her mother's friend, Edith, coming from a nearby cottage.

"Father, you know these young folks from Covehithe, the Village in the Morning Sun," Edith said. "We see them every summer at the gathering." She turned to them. "Norsemen in Covehithe? Tell me."

"Edith, I was talking to them first." The old man's querulous voice protested the interruption.

"I know, Father. You remember Catla and Sven. We have to listen."

Relief made Catla's body sag, and her voice shook as she reached out and clutched Edith's arm. "Edith, you have to help us! Nord-devils burned Covehithe last day after sunup." The words tumbled out of Catla's mouth. "I was on the heath so I didn't get caught, but the cottages are burning. Men in black tunics came in a warship." Catla watched Edith's eyes widen as she listened. "Sven and I saw them again today on land and in their ship. They're coming here, up the river. You're in danger." Catla pulled Edith's arm closer before she said, "And Edith, I don't know what's happened to my family."

Edith reached over and gathered her into her arms. "Hush, hush, now. We'll help you." As Wulfric sounded a metal hoop to gather the villagers, she said, "But softly, Father. We don't want to alert our enemies."

"Ach, they'll not hear it on the water. They'll be fighting the rapids about now."

"Norsemen! Norsemen on the river! Council! Council!" Wulfric shouted with the authority of someone who was used to being obeyed. Edith settled Catla and Sven while she went back into her cottage. People came, everyone talking at once. A small boy spat at Sven and got a cuff on his back from his mother. A little girl sidled up to Catla and said, "Your name is Catla, isn't it? Your mother fixed my dolly last summer. I remember you."

"I remember you too, Mathilda." But Catla could not think about dolls. She gently turned Mathilda back toward her mother as Edith appeared with some flat bread and two horns of ale.

Wulfric roared for quiet. "These two, Catla and Sven, asked for a council. They need help, and they bring a warning. They've seen Norsemen on the river today."

Sven started to speak, but Edith said, "Wait. People need to settle. You two. Sit there under the oak." She pointed to some three-legged stools. "Eat and drink a little." She turned to the villagers and said, "Council, is this the kind of order you bring to a council ring?" The villagers shuffled into a rough circle, sitting on the ground or on logs and stumps as the talking subsided.

"I didn't recognize you," Wulfric said to Catla and Sven. "Now I see you are from Covehithe. I was too gruff. It's my old-man eyes."

"And your old-man bark," Edith said. She patted his arm affectionately. "Now, Catla, you have the place of speech. We'll hear your story."

As Edith spoke, a tall man with a gray beard and a head covering of felted wool moved toward them. The people parted to allow him room and nodded to him in respect. He strode forward, his stave in his right hand.

"That's Hugh, Edith's husband," Wulfric said to Catla. "He's the headman and has the gift. He'll listen and judge your tale."

Sven and Catla knew Hugh. They bobbed their heads in a small bow to him. Sven poked Catla in the ribs to urge her to start.

"Last day, before short shadow, Nord-devils came and set fire to Covehithe." She paused and waited for the gasps and exclamations to end. "There was smoke everywhere. They herded people toward our goat pen." She stood suddenly to emphasize her words. "What if they're taken and sold as slaves? I'll never see them again. Come back with us. Help us!" Then suddenly she could say no more, as if all her air had been pushed out of her.

The villagers turned to their neighbors and a hubbub of talk started again. Someone called out, "Did you see Sarah?"

"Was anyone killed?" another voice asked.

The iron ring sounded again, but more softly this time, and everyone looked at Hugh.

"Order." His face was hard as he looked at Catla. "We've not seen a slave raid for years. The Norse ships didn't bother us on their way to the battles by York. But then they were defeated. They could be trying to make up their war losses with some slaves. Grim news, indeed. How many men are there?"

Sven took up the story and answered Hugh's question first. "I think more than ten, but we didn't count." Then he spoke to the rest of the gathering. "Catla saw this, not I. I was in York yesterday. I found her sleeping at the standing stones last night on her way here. No one travels at night unless they are hard pressed. Covehithe needs you."

Sven opened his mouth to continue, but Catla

broke in. "There's more. On this day, not long after sunup, we saw Nord-devils beside the hill, the one with the elders on top. They got into their ship and pulled into the river, coming this way. They're the men who invaded Covehithe. They'll take you for slaves too. Your families will be torn apart. Our villages will disappear. They're coming here." Catla almost yelled the last words in her urgency to have them come with her, back to Covehithe, now. Why didn't they move?

A new babble of voices arose until Wulfric raised his right arm for order. "Quiet. Quiet, I say. Are we a council or not? Act like a council and think. Listen. Hugh will guide us through our plan."

People fell silent as Hugh moved forward. "Covehithe is in desperate trouble. They need our help. That much is very clear. We'll help them. We'll be attacked soon though, and then we will see the good of our plan. First, we must protect the children. Mothers, gather whatever you need to take the children to the hill fort. Leave quickly, as soon as you're ready. Then we'll finish preparing for the Norsemen. After that, we'll help our neighbors in Covehithe."

Catla listened but didn't understand what he meant about a hill fort and a plan prepared for the Norsemen. She did understand Covehithe would get help, but she didn't know when. She wanted it to be now.

CHAPTER SIX

Setting the Trap

As Hugh finished speaking, a group of boys around Sven's age appeared from behind the cottage closest to the river's edge. Edith plucked Wulfric's sleeve to move him aside, and the boys strode into the circle. A red-haired one said, "We heard a call to council, but there was one last knot to tie. Sorry to be late." Their wide smiles showed white teeth against their dirty faces.

Catla recognized Fergus, whom she knew from the Longest Day celebrations, but she wasn't sure who the others were. Sweat formed muddy paths down their foreheads and cheeks so it was hard to tell.

Hugh smiled back and said, "Good reason to be late, Fergus. Are you lads finished?"

Fergus glanced around the ring of people, about to speak, when his eyes rested on Catla. "Catla, greetings, and to you too, Sven." His voice went high with surprise. "What brings you to our part of the world?" But he didn't wait for an answer. He turned to Hugh. "Yes! We are finished."

The villagers' faces lit with excitement. A loud cheer went up, and they hugged each other, grabbed children and danced in circles.

"Good work, boys!"

"Not a whisker too soon."

"Now we're ready for the barbarians."

Catla looked at Sven to see if he knew what they were talking about, but he shrugged.

Sven tugged at Fergus's sleeve, but Fergus jerked his arm away and turned again to Hugh. "What's this about? We thought the council wanted a report on the work, but I see Catla and my friend here. Something's going on."

"It's somber news. Covehithe was attacked last day," Hugh said. "Norsemen have taken the people prisoner and the village burns. Catla and Sven seek our help. They saw a Norse ship this day headed upriver toward us. They think it's the same men who overran Covehithe."

Catla's body stiffened to hear Hugh speak of her home. It made the events more real, and she felt a little sick while she listened.

"Sven, Catla, that's terrible," Fergus said. "This changes things." He called to the villagers. "No, I've seen no Norse ship on the river this day."

"Good," Hugh said. "Erik, go stand watch. Come immediately if you see a ship. The Norsemen left Elder Bush Hill and are heading upriver. They have a ways to travel, but we need a watch."

One of the boys, freckles showing faintly through the dirt, turned and ran.

Catla wanted to see for herself. "Hugh, how long will they take? Sven and I got here so fast."

"The path is faster," Hugh said, "and they're rowing against the tide and some rapids. They'll be slow with so few of them at the oars. Downriver there's a shoal that shifts around in the river so it will be tricky. Beyond the shoal, the riverbed holds rocky ridges. They're in for some nasty surprises." His voice rose as he addressed the villagers. "And we have another for them, don't we?"

The villagers shouted their agreement.

"All right. Let's get on with things," Hugh said. "Edith, you'll organize the women and children for the hill fort? They'll stay there while we're at Covehithe, so five days should do it. You'll need food and— well, you know what to do."

"I will and I do." Then Edith said to Catla, "You are of the age where we give people the choice to stay here to face danger or to go to the hill fort. I imagine I know what you'd rather do."

"Yes, I'll stay. But thank you, Edith, for not choosing for me."

"I thought as much. I'd do the same. Come to my cottage, anytime, to rest or visit."

Catla's eyes smarted at the kindness. "Edith, thank you. I'll find you." She blinked the tears away.

"Now, Sven and Catla," Hugh said, "Fergus is going to show you our surprise."

Fergus swept his arm across his body in a low bow indicating they should go first down the river path. "Remember at the Longest Day this summer there was much talk about Norse ships in our waters?" They nodded and he continued. "When we got home, our council decided to take action. We've built a trap." He paused. "A trap for rats."

"A trap?" Sven burst out. "How?"

"Ha! You'll see. The Norsemen are not the only ones to sell slaves. Our king pays well for oarsmen. We're turning the game around."

Catla was dumbfounded. It never occurred to her that Nord-devils could be captured. Fergus swept his hand toward the river. "There it is. What do you think?"

Catla tried to figure out what she was seeing. Nets hung over the cliff's edge, braced by tree trunks.

The nets held rocks and dirt, with shrubs and bushes on the bottom holding everything in place. It all blended into the cliff side right next to the path coming from the river. "How does it work?" she asked.

"On each side of the path a rope joins two sections of nets. When the ropes are pulled away…"

"Everything falls on top of the Nord-devils." Catla's excitement burst out into a little dance. "I see how it works. That's clever, Fergus!"

Fergus smiled and said, "You have it! This one has brains and beauty, eh, Sven?"

Catla felt her cheeks grow hot at the words.

Sven scowled but said, "Well, I'll be a boar's tusk!"

"Me too," said Catla.

"Ha, you hope it works," said a voice behind them. Wulfric had been standing, listening. "That's the plan, but it's not been tested yet."

Catla thought Wulfric sounded like he was carrying on a long-standing argument.

"That's true, Wulfric." Fergus spoke with respect. "We wanted to test it, like you said, but now the test will be in the action. You showed us the way to set the trees though."

Wulfric's frown disappeared. "There were some rare old tumbles."

"Yes, that's true. Matthew and Wulfric showed us how to tie knots that will release when they're pulled."

"But you're just coming to the best part, Fergus. Tell them what happens after we drop the dirt on the rats." Almost in spite of himself, Wulfric seemed to be entering into the spirit of the story.

Catla smiled at the old man. He reminded her of her grandfather, who, even after he'd given the leadership of the village to his son, still wanted to run things.

"After the rocks and dirt crash down, we'll flip the nets off the poles onto the enemy," Fergus said. "It's our only hope against their weapons and skill."

Catla felt an involuntary shudder as she recalled the axes and swords.

"Our fishermen will fling their nets over everything. Hey, there they are." Fergus waved to the men who were gathering nets beside their boats at the waterside. "They're folding them so they'll spread wide, not stay in a clump. Takes years of practice."

"I was told to bring you folks for food and rest before the excitement," Wulfric said. Then he muttered, "If there is any."

Catla looked at him sharply. "Don't you think they'll come?"

"Oh, they'll come," he said. "Ignore me. Everyone is carrying on, but Edith has decided I'm to go to the hill fort. Says someone has to be in charge up there. I know the real reason. She's worried I won't be able to keep up on the way to Covehithe."

"Oh, Wulfric," Catla said. She reached over and gave him a quick hug. "You remind me of my grandfather."

"Your grandfather, eh? A great man," he said. He straightened his shoulders and took Catla's arm. "You'd better come. The wagons are nearly loaded, and Edith is worried you're too tired. Fergus, you're to stay with Erik and share the watch."

"I'll stay as well, Wulfric," said Sven. "You're all right, aren't you, Catla?"

Catla nodded and walked with Wulfric, thinking about the villagers' daring. If only the people of Covehithe had thought of a trap. She felt new tears forming. Then she lifted her head and sent her village a quick prayer. She would keep hope. As if he sensed her struggle, Wulfric patted her hand.

Catla said, "Tell me about the hill fort. I've never heard of it before."

"It's less than half a day's walk north of the standing stones," he said. "Everyone in these parts knows of it— I'm sure your parents do—but I doubt the Norsemen are aware it exists. It's old, built on a hill, and we've fixed the ruins of buildings on top. There are several ditches circling it, to slow down invaders. We keep animals there in bad weather. It's a safe spot for the children now."

When they joined Edith and Hugh, Edith said, "The last time the lord's steward came by, he said the hill fort was in good repair and the well was working, so there's good water. An ancient people built it, around the time of the standing stones or maybe later. Before the Romans came. It's easy to defend. When we started building the trap, we decided at council that the children, their mothers and the older folks would be safer at the hill fort." She stepped closer to Hugh, looked him in the eye and said, "I'll go along for a short way, Hugh, to see them on the right path, but I'm coming back. I want to see the trap sprung."

Hugh looked as though he wanted to argue, but he nodded instead.

"I'd like to see the hill fort someday," Catla said, "but right now I'd like to help." She looked at the wooden wagons piled with food, pots and sleeping robes. Some crates holding chickens were piled on one wagon. They'd be food for the foxes if they were left behind. She thought about the villagers separated from their loved ones in this time of danger. But they'd be safe from capture, she reminded herself.

One woman complained loudly to a dark-haired man who must have been her husband. "Why can't we stay? I'd be here with him. He's four years old. He'll not get in the way. He knows how to mind what I say. I want to stay and fight. You know I'm good with my stave."

Edith took her arm and spoke to her softly.

The woman jerked her arm away and finished putting the items piled on the ground beside her onto a cart. "Come along then, Egbert." A small boy climbed up on top of the pile and the dark-haired man gave both his wife and child a kiss.

"She's right, you know," Wulfric said at Catla's side where he had watched the same scene. "Everyone wants to be here for the fight."

Edith looked at him from across the path and said, "It is hard for you to go, Father."

"Yes, it is. But someone has to be in charge. I've had a lot of experience. I'll make sure everything is all right up there."

"Thank you, Father. That is important to us all."

Catla kept her eyes on the ground to hide her smile at Wulfric's capitulation. She was glad she'd had this chance to know him a little. She'd look for him at the next Longest Day celebration—if there was one.

One of the young women said, "My friends and I will go and help our mothers settle the children and grandparents. But we want to go to Covehithe, so we'll meet you at the standing stones. Can one of the boys come and tell us when you're leaving? He could bring everyone news of the ambush."

Hugh said, "Yes, Brida, good idea. You shall come. I promise we'll send for you and any others who want to join us at Covehithe."

Brida called to Hindley, the village cooper. "Father, did you hear that? I'm to go to Covehithe. Hugh said so, just now."

Hindley walked over to his daughter and said, "I'd rather you were staying safe, but I know how much you want to be there. You have my blessing, child."

The twisty paths between the cottages filled with scurrying folks. Women's voices called to each other.

"I've got a few peas left."

"I'll bring the bread I made."

"I've got a pot of food ready, but I'll leave some behind too."

People worked and chattered to each other, everyone intent on getting the jobs done.

Catla backed away until her legs felt the small stool beside Edith's cottage wall. She watched the bustling scene and all at once thought about home. What was her family doing right now? Were the Nord-devils giving them anything to drink or eat? Were the children safe?

Everything was taking too long here. She wanted to leave for Covehithe now. She shook her hair across her face to hide her resentment. She knew she was being petty. Moment by moment she felt a deep isolation. Surrounded by friendly faces, she still felt much alone.

CHAPTER SEVEN

A Swift Turn of Events

A haze of fine dust floating in the air above the bustling village caught the rays of the sun. It settled on the villagers eating bread with porridge. Some of them ate newly harvested onions, and everyone had some ale. Catla hadn't felt hungry, but when Edith appeared with a smear of porridge on bread and an onion, her stomach rumbled.

Edith smiled at the sound. "Eat now, Catla. No one has forgotten Covehithe. The hill-fort group is almost ready to leave."

Eating made Catla feel guilty. Her family was hungry and suffering, and she had food and freedom. She looked into the blue autumn sky. Its calm provided a sharp contrast to the activity all around her. Suddenly, she felt exhausted and became aware again of the throbbing in her sore leg. She was glad for the sun-warmed wall and leaned against it as she watched bundles of fur and food grow higher.

Sven came around the corner of the cottage, his shirt gathered like a bag, holding stones. "For the Norsemen," he said. At her questioning look, he explained, "We're making piles of rocks to throw at the Norsemen. They're all along the path." He crouched beside her and chewed the bread Edith handed him. When he finished eating, he patted Catla's arm awkwardly and left.

The village dogs with wide chests and long legs were harnessed to the wagons with leather thongs and traces. Catla was used to these snarling, growling beasts, but she was glad that they were muzzled.

Wulfric passed, holding the elbow of an older woman who moved with difficulty. He treated her tenderly, and Catla could see why Edith had wanted him at the hill fort.

"Leah, here's a place on these soft wolf pelts," Edith said. Leah settled herself on one of the wagons and lifted her arms to hold a baby. Mathilda and another toddler climbed up beside her.

One of the younger boys appeared with two milk goats harnessed together.

"Good thinking, Daniel. You'll need nanny goats. I see you have tied them well." Edith bent to examine the knots that held the goats, and Daniel's face glowed under the praise.

"I've let the rest out to graze. We'll find them when we come home. Matthew told me to let the pigs find their own food too."

"Well done, Daniel." Hugh patted his shoulder.

Mathilda had skidded off the slippery bedding robes and was crying. Wulfric picked her up, gave her a short hug, then settled her on a shorter pile beside a knot, which he put in her hand. Holding her doll among the folded furs, she waved to Catla and called, "We're going on an adventure, Catla. I'm holding on to this knot."

Catla smiled at her, but suddenly tears threatened to spill. She stammered out a faint, "Good luck," and turned her face away, afraid she'd cry if she looked at the eager little girl any longer. Her red cheeks and trusting eyes reminded her too much of Bega.

Hugh moved among the women and children, speaking quietly, stooping to tighten a rope here or tuck in a piece of fur there. "Brida, you'll lead? You know the way? Wulfric will point you straight if you need help." Hugh draped his arm over Edith's shoulders and pressed her close in a short hug. "Thank you. I'll see you soon." Then he faced the assembly. "Thank you for your quick work. Go in safety with blessings until we meet again." The small procession of walkers and four wagons set off toward the haven in the hills.

Hugh turned to Catla. "I'm glad you are resting. You're tired."

"I suppose I am."

"Edith will go part of the way and then come back. She likes a good fight, and she doesn't want to miss the Norsemen."

Catla smiled at this fierce side of the woman who treated her so gently. She closed her eyes and tried to envision Covehithe as it had been, with everyone safe and happy. Then she moved her mind forward to see into the future. She'd meet with the women in their circle at the next Longest Day celebration. Girls were invited after their eleventh summer. She'd been invited last summer but hadn't been interested. Now that she was thirteen and almost betrothed, she'd be expected. She wished she had gone last summer. Maybe she'd know better what to do about Olav.

The next thing she felt was wolf fur tickling her nose. She rolled over and saw she was on a pile of sleeping robes inside a cottage. She stretched and sat up, lifting her skirt to check her sore leg. The bruise was turning yellow at the edges and was less tender when she touched it.

Outside the cottage, people were talking. She listened. Had the Nord-devils come?

No one shouted. Nothing seemed wrong.

She left the cottage and approached the council circle.

"How do you feel?" Hugh asked. "Better?"

"Yes, I do. Was I asleep long?"

"Not long. I was afraid you'd topple off the little stool, so I moved you inside."

"Thank you. What's happening now?"

Hugh gestured to some weapons lying on the ground. "We've collected all the village weapons. Everyone needs to be armed, including you, Catla. You can choose when the villagers are done."

She felt for her catapult in the pouch which hung beside her drinking horn, and wished for her own short knife. She eyed a slim stave of ash. She'd choose it, if someone didn't take it first, and a knife, if one were left.

"Peter, you've got your short sword," Hugh said. "Go stand watch and send the boys back to choose their weapons." Peter nodded and trotted off.

Hugh touched his sword. "I've got what I need. Matthew, have you got yours?"

"Aye, and I'm keeping it too," Matthew growled.

"Fair enough. Claim your weapons, everyone," Hugh said. "Edith has her knife, stave and catapult with her." In the end, three skinning knives and a few staves, including the one Catla liked, were left.

"Catla, choose a knife and a stave."

"All right, Hugh. I like this stave. It's not too heavy." With a knife in her belt and a stave in hand, she swallowed hard, hoping she was ready, hoping she would know what to do when the Nord-devils came.

Fergus explained the strategy. "Lie on the path behind the plants and bushes, close to a pile of throwing stones. Pelt them with the rocks after I give the signal. You men who are the pullers, position yourself beside the ropes."

Several men shifted next to each other. Catla focused on Fergus.

"When they land," Fergus continued, "let them get close to the oak sapling on the upriver side of the path. That's when you rope-pullers will release the ambush. The rest of you, throw your rocks as hard as you can. Really pelt them! Then the nets will trap them."

Hugh said, "Good, Fergus. We'll follow you." Then he turned a somber face to the people of his village and said, "Our lives and those of our friends in Covehithe are at risk. This is the way we will win. They have better weapons, and killing is what they're trained to do. We put in our military time fighting for our king and lord, but mainly we are peaceable folks, but clever. It's wits, not weapons, that will win this day."

Villagers elbowed each other and smiled grimly. Catla wished she could smile, but her mouth would not budge.

"To the cliffs!" Hugh's voice was calm and firm. "Be wary. They'll believe we are easy pickings, after taking Covehithe so easily, so they'll be confident. But when they're caught by the nets they'll be angry, so stay out of reach of their weapons."

Catla turned to the river path, her eyes searching for stones to add to the cache in her apron. The knot in the pit of her stomach was back, and her heart knocked against her ribs. Her eyes sought Sven, but he was not looking her way. Then her resolve took hold and her mind steadied. She would show everyone that Athelstan and Sarah's daughter had valor.

Peter arrived, red-faced with excitement. "They're coming up the river," he called in a hoarse whisper. "They're closing on our beach."

"Into position. Out of sight. Lie still!" Hugh took command. "Let them think we're napping."

Fergus silently pointed Catla to her place and others followed his directions. Like shadows, they stooped and crept to their spots. Flat on her belly, she peered down to the river, the beach and the ship drawing close.

Her mouth was dry, and a shiver coursed through her body.

Catla selected a stone from the pile by her head and held it, easing her catapult into her other hand. The river sparkled. Terns called and wheeled against the sky. The actions of the Norsemen seemed doubly grim on such a peaceful day. But so it had been last day on the heath. She whispered a hurried prayer for everyone to be safe. Her ears thumped with the beat of her heart and her shoulders tightened.

The long ship turned with a sweep of the oars and drifted toward them.

Out of the breeze, the sail flapped like an old shawl. The red stripes were clear against the silt brown of the river. Sunlight glinted off the knobs of metal pounded into each black shield, piled in the bottom of the ship. Leather helmets and leather straps covered the invaders' faces, shading their eyes.

One sweep of the oars brought the ship to the beach.

CHAPTER EIGHT

The Eyes of the Dragon

The rasp of scraped pebbles carried clearly in the still air as the Norse ship landed by the water's edge.

Catla's throat felt full of grit. Flattened into the worn hollow of the path, she peered between a juniper bush and some feverfew, her mind racing with questions. Could they defeat the Nord-devils? What if she died? Or Sven? She blinked to erase the fear. She recalled her father's words: *Hold a clear image of the end result you want—then work to make it so.* She pictured her family together, Bega on her lap, her chin resting on Bega's head. She gripped her rock and catapult and stared at the ship.

Arching heads—half dragon, half snake, sinuous and lithe—reared from both bow and stern. The sound of villagers sucking in their breath comforted her. She was not alone. Her eyes focused on the dragon-heads. Some people believed it was the eyes of the dragon that sought out villages to burn and rob.

Her father had roared with laughter when she'd told him that. "Nonsense," he'd said. "Nonsense." She smiled at the memory but ducked her head and lowered her gaze, unwilling now to take his word.

At new sounds, she looked up again. The Nord-devils sat on rowing benches in the wide bilge. Some of them scooped up their shields and vaulted over the side into knee-deep water. They pulled the shallow, rounded hull onto the land. It tilted on its keel and everyone clambered out.

Two Nord-devils kicked at the small leather fishing boats, overturned and drying on the pebbled beach. One slashed at the leather hulls and muttered harsh-sounding words. Sword hilts protruded from leather scabbards. Knives flashed at belted waists. Some men carried axes. Catla peered at their weapons and black tunics. She thought they were the same men she'd seen below Elder Bush Hill and in her village, although their faces were obscured by their helmets. Snatches of muted laughter floated up from the path. The Nord-devils huddled close together, but they seemed relaxed and confident, unaware of the trap.

One man said something, his words sounding as harsh as a seal's bark, and they turned and looked toward the villagers. Fear held Catla's body rigid. She heard no outcry. The villagers had not been seen. She ducked her head slightly, her heart pounding. A man jerked his head toward the ship and two others shook their heads as if to argue, but they turned and climbed back into the ship, likely for lookout duty. That might be a problem. They all had to be captured.

Catla was so absorbed in the scene below, she almost shrieked when someone slid in beside her. The whisper of a familiar voice brushed her cheek. "Easy. Be calm. I thought you might like company. This must remind you of home."

She turned and saw the kindness in Edith's face, then nodded her head once, hard. Dropping her rock for an instant, she put her hand into Edith's, squeezed it and felt the answering pressure. Some of the tension in her back eased. Edith settled her catapult in front of her within easy reach and they turned to watch.

The Nord-devils formed a close, silent cluster as they advanced up the path to the village, forming a wall of shields. Catla remembered a traveler talking about such a thing, and her father said he, too, had fought like that. Catla fixed her eyes on them and tightened her fingers on her stone. The sun glittered off the flat planes of the axes. The sword blades glinted as they slashed at low-growing bushes. She felt a nervous tremble as she thought of the ambush of stones and bushes matched against their enemy's weapons and warrior skill. The invaders came closer, their helmets hiding their eyes, their shields at chest level.

The trap would only work if the Nord-devils stayed close together. Her eyes kept snaking between Fergus and the men below as the invaders drew closer. They were almost at the oak sapling. Were they too close? She shifted her eyes and fastened them on Fergus. He signaled and picked up the rope. The silence held. The rope-pullers jumped up, braced their feet and pulled. Muscles bulged; the ropes stretched tight. For an instant nothing moved. Nord-devils would swarm over the river cliff and look straight into her eyes. The men heaved again.

Abruptly, the netting parted.

Catla jumped to her feet as the dirt, rocks, boulders and bushes plummeted onto the enemy, filling their eyes and mouths. She flung her rocks, aiming for the open flesh of their arms and faces. The boulders and rocks bounced off the Nord-devils' helmets and backs and tumbled down the incline to the shoreline.

They lurched and scrambled, trying to stay on their feet. Loose rocks tripped them. They cut each other as they swung their swords to keep their balance. Shields clashed. The air resounded with cries, curses and snarls.

Then the fishermen flung their nets. The rope-pullers dropped the slack ropes over the edge of the riverbank for later. Villagers hurled rock after rock. The empty nets flipped down over top of the Nord-devils, who howled, struggled and shouted in rage, ensnared in the nets, a seething mass of tangled arms and legs. Norse curses vied with shouts of triumph from the villagers when a rock struck a target.

Catla couldn't keep track of everything that happened. From the moment when the invaders had been so close to the villagers, to when the nets had caught them, she'd hardly taken a breath. Now she realized all her rocks had been thrown. She leaped about and shouted in joy, until Edith reminded her their job was not done.

Catla slithered down the bank with the rest of the villagers. The rope-pullers wound the ropes around the netted Norsemen, then pulled both ends tighter and tighter, drawing the Nord-devils closer together. The invaders scuffled and shifted as the ropes pressed them inward. Yells and curses filled the air. The trap was working. Catla shifted her grip on her stave, checked that her knife was still in her belt. Now her heart pounded in excitement, not fear.

The invaders used their knives to hack at the webbing. The villagers used their staves to knock the weapons away from the prisoners' hands and jabbed at them through the netting. A few villagers picked up the fallen weapons, until Hugh bellowed, "Leave them. You're too close. Some still have their knives and swords. We'll get them later."

Catla had been eyeing a short sword with an intricate hilt, but she backed away from it when Hugh spoke. The ropes were pulled and the trap tightened.

When the Norsemen were a tight bundle, the villagers claimed the fallen weapons. Catla darted in and picked up the sword she'd seen. *I'll take it home. Maybe Bega will like it when she grows older*. She smiled and tucked it into her belt.

The prisoners' struggles slowed. Catla was reminded of a net full of squirming black smelts. Hugh bellowed for quiet, but a few of the villagers continued to poke at the prisoners with their staves.

"That's for my brother," one man yelled. He thrust his stave into an opening. "He was a good man, taken one winter evening when he was alone."

Others cheered, jabbed and called out the names of family members and friends who had gone missing in slave raids. Catla was looking for an opening for her own stave when Hugh raised his arms again. "Stop! Stop now. These men will be slaves. Don't blind or maim them. They need to be strong to bring a goodly price."

The jabbing and jeering stopped.

Hugh said, "Good work, everyone. Good work! Let's get them to the council ring."

A cheer burst from the crowd of villagers.

Then Hugh yelled something in Norse. Catla wasn't surprised that he knew some words of Norse. She remembered her father saying that part of Hugh's family had helped build York over one hundred years ago.

There were more struggles from within the net, more jabbing and whacking with staves. At last, one Norse voice rose above the growls and snarls, and the struggles stopped.

More cheers filled the air. Catla's voice was drowned in the tumult.

"They've been told to drop out their weapons and stand still," Hugh said. "When you see a weapon, whoever is closest, run and pick it up. Be on guard. They'll try to keep their knives."

"Do we get to keep the weapons, Hugh?" asked Hindley.

"Yes, we'll keep them and divide them by the oak tree. The spoils of war will be shared equally."

Catla wasn't the only one who coveted a strong and skill-fully made Norse weapon.

Angry words still came from inside the net, but slowly knives and swords appeared through the webbing and dropped to the ground. After the last knife dropped, the villagers darted in and pulled the weapons away. The Norsemen stood still. The villagers raised another cheer, slapped their neighbors' backs and pranced about in glee and relief.

Catla danced too, her heart filled with joy.

The mighty Nord-devils were captured. There was hope for Covehithe.

One Norseman at a time was untangled from the net, searched for weapons, and bound, hands and feet, with thin strands of hide. He could take short steps but would topple if he tried to run. More short knives were discovered, and the men who had hidden them received a whack for their trickery.

Then Catla remembered the ship in the harbor and the two guards. She looked at the river and her mouth dropped open in surprise. "Sven!" she yelled. Other people turned to the ship and saw two more prisoners sitting in the bilge, their bodies wrapped with rope. Sven and three friends stood behind them, short stab-bing knives at the ready. Catla realized she hadn't seen Sven during the fight. She was glad he was safe but felt miffed she hadn't been told about his plan. Then she chided herself. He was with his friends, the older boys. He didn't need to tell her his plans.

"How did you do that?" Matthew called to the boys in the ship. He sounded cross too. "Oh, never mind. Good work. Bring them here with the others and we'll hear about it later."

Catla waved and Sven waved back. She grinned when she heard Matthew complaining to Hindley that the boys hadn't told him what they were planning. It reminded her of Wulfric. No one liked to miss out on things, not even her.

The boys hoisted the captives to their feet and then all the invaders shuffled up the path to the village.

As Catla walked to council ring, Hugh said, "Put them into the goat pen for now." The goat pen? In her mind's eye, she saw her family pushed toward their own pen. Her hope for justice grew. These people of Aigber were more resourceful than she had dared to count on.

Catla waited until most of the villagers climbed the riverbank before she did. As she headed to the council ring, a movement between the cottages caught her eye. One of the invaders raced down the path out of the village. Matthew and Hugh bellowed. Fergus and Sven sprinted behind the invader. People shouted, "Stop him! Stop him!"

Fergus pulled his knife from his belt as he ran. He was ahead of Sven by a leg-length, closing on the fugitive.

"Go, Fergus!" Sven's voice broke the silence.

Catla darted forward, caught in the drama.

The Norseman sprinted between cottages and started along the path to the heath. As he passed her, she realized with a shock that he was about her age. The long leather strand that had hobbled him flipped around one leg. His face contorted in desperation. He veered off the path and dodged a low blackberry bramble, evading Fergus. The thong whipped around his opposite ankle. His body twisted as he tried to maintain balance, but he stumbled. His arms were still bound behind his back and he came down heavily on his shoulder.

Catla caught the glint of a blade in his hand as he sprawled on his side in the dirt. Fergus and Sven were too close to stop. They landed on top of him, Fergus first, then Sven. There was no struggle. Sven pushed himself up and lowered his hand to Fergus, who pushed himself away from the boy, grabbed Sven's hand and stood. The Norseman lay still. Blood glistened on Fergus's knife and hand, and his face was pale. It was not clear to Catla if Fergus had meant to stab the prisoner or not. The crowd fell silent.

One of the men said, "Good for you, lad."

Matthew said, "He deserved what he got."

"Is he dead?" Fergus asked.

Catla's stomach lurched.

Edith and Hugh knelt beside the boy, and the crowd encircled them. Edith examined the cut. "He still lives, but not for long," she said. "The knife caught his neck. The cut is very deep. He cannot be saved. He'll die quickly."

"Bring his lord before he dies," Hugh said. Sven turned, but Erik and Rufus had already gone.

The news had a sobering effect. This village shared Father John as their priest, and he preached "Thou shalt not kill." It was a mortal sin to take another person's life, but this was war. Some of the villagers crossed themselves. Some crossed their fingers and spat on the ground. All believed a lost soul could haunt their village if it did not find peace. Catla wondered if the warrior would find his way to his Norse heaven, Valhalla. She shivered in pity for both Fergus and the Norseman.

The Norse chief arrived, and Hugh cut his hands free so he could comfort the boy. He spoke softly and closed the young man's fingers more firmly around the knife still in his hand. He crossed the boy's arms over his chest. Made a sign on his forehead.

Hugh translated what the chief had said. "This one will find peace. He died with his knife in his hand, as a true warrior should. He will feast in Odin's hall."

The young man's chest grew still. Matthew and Rufus retied the chief's hands and took him back to the goat pen.

Some men picked up the body and went to dig a grave. Edith went to find a piece of cloth for the wrapping. A few of the women offered to bring rocks to place on the disturbed earth of his grave. Fresh blood would attract the wolves, and that night the village would be empty.

CHAPTER NINE

Turning Toward home

Catla joined the villagers gathered in the council ring. The young Norseman's death had shocked her. Dunstan, Cuthbert and Bega were smaller and younger. They would die even more quickly. Her heart ached with fear for her family. How precarious life was and how quickly taken. Death was the true spoil of war.

The excitement of the victory filled the air with chatter and laughter. The villagers' high spirits made her feel bleak. *Your families are safe*, she thought. But these new friends were not to blame for her gloomy thoughts. Without their plan, this moment would be very different. There'd be no hope at all.

Hindley grabbed her around the waist, lifted her off her feet and whirled around the council ring, singing "La-la-la." Everyone laughed. At first she protested but quickly saw there was happiness enough to share, so she relaxed and sang too. Hindley grinned and winked when she smiled.

Ale beakers passed from hand to hand. Hugh said, "A drink. A drink to a job well done." A clamor of voices swelled in triumph.

"We showed them," Matthew hollered.

"And they thought they were so tough!"

"They were lambs." Hindley bleated his last word. His cry echoed around the ring as many voices bleated in agreement.

Catla found a stump to sit on as she sipped from her drinking horn and considered the way these villagers called the invaders Norsemen, not Nord-devils. And they had won a victory against them. Norseman sounded less powerful, less evil and more ordinary than Nord-devil. Would her fear be less if she called them Norsemen? She resolved to stop saying Nord-devils. They could die and be outwitted, like everyone else. They had no evil powers.

She raised her horn and whooped in joy and thanksgiving, shouting, "The Norsemen will be defeated." Her voice was lost in the racket, but it didn't matter.

She'd said it and it felt right. Men clapped each other's backs, and women hugged. Catla felt new hope, enthusiasm and trust.

Hugh called for attention. "We'll divide the Norse weapons equally. Ah, Edith, there you are." He put his arm around his wife's shoulders and gave her a squeeze. "I thought I tasted your ale. Good. Will you divide the weapons?"

At Edith's nod, he said, "Does anyone oppose Edith making the decisions or want to help?" He paused, but no one spoke.

Catla sat and watched as people circled Edith and the stack of weapons. The tree sheltered them from the western sun and dappled their faces as their eyes focused on the jumbled mass of weapons. Edith handed Sven a short stabbing knife and gave him another to pass to Catla. It was the one she had first picked up. Edith smiled when Catla called her thanks.

Hugh said, "Edith, are you putting extra weapons aside for those who are not here?"

Edith's eyes smiled as she looked up at him and said, "Yes, m'lord." She made a slight bow. People laughed. They'd noticed the other pile of weapons by her side.

Hugh looked slightly abashed. He squeezed her shoulders and said, "It's hard to get ahead of you, m'lady." A few people chuckled because Hugh seldom made an error. He only called her m'lady for a bit of a joke, even though everyone knew Hugh and Edith were welcomed at court and she was entitled to the honor. Catla watched the easy manner they had with each other. They were not fierce like her parents were sometimes. Their voices held respect and care, and smiles were often ready on their faces. She wished her marriage, when it came, would be like that. Olav didn't fit Hugh's pattern, and while she worried about what she would find when she got back to Covehithe, she remembered her vow to marry him if her family was safe. Even so, the idea made her slightly queasy. She pushed the thought aside and wished she were on her way home. Everything was dragging, and every minute her family was held captive was a minute too long.

When the weapons were dispersed, someone said, "What about the women and children at the hill fort? They'll want to know what's happened and that we're about to leave."

"Theodore's already gone," Hugh said.

Catla was surprised that Hugh had chosen Theodore. She thought he was too young, even though he was tall for eleven summers.

Then Edith said, "Good choice. He's young but he knows the land. He's worked with the herders and shepherds for the last few years. Good with his catapult too."

Matthew, his father, nodded his agreement and said, "I won't boast, but he's a canny lad." People smiled their approval. Obviously no one else was worried that Theodore was too young for the job.

Hugh said, "He and Brida will join us at the standing stones tonight. Wulfric will stay at the hill fort and see to things there. Are we still in agreement to sell our invading guests to the king?" The word *guests* was spun out with a twist and brought a loud laugh.

"Some guests! Who invited *them*?" Hindley quipped as he spun around and pointed at Catla. "Did you?"

"No, no, of course not," Catla sputtered, flinging her hands up in protest. Then she laughed along with the rest of the villagers at the ridiculous idea.

"String them all up by their necks," someone shouted.

"Sell them," Matthew said.

Catla struggled with her feelings as she listened to the debate. She feared the invaders and hated them for raiding her village. The smoke and flames rolled into her mind's eye along with the small figure clutching the woman's leg. Her mouth suddenly had a sour taste. But did she want them killed? Hugh had shown compassion and respect by bringing their leader to the dying man. But they were still the enemy.

"I thought we'd agreed we'd do that too," Fergus said.

"Murdering heathens!" Hindley yelled.

"Dead men don't make good slaves," Hugh said. "This raiding party is likely part of the Covehithe group. I'm guessing the leader of this group is not acting on their king's orders."

"How could he be? Their king died on the battlefield," Matthew said. "Most of them have gone home with their wounded."

"It appears," said Hindley, "that some of them 'forgot' to go home. They'd be the ones in the goat pen." Jeers and laughter followed his words.

Catla's head swam as she tried to keep up with the various opinions. She wanted to yell, *Just get on with it! This is nonsense! Covehithe needs us*. But she didn't. Hugh knew speed was important. She needed patience. She dug her fingers into the palms of her clenched fists in an effort to be still.

"They'll make good slaves! We'd be fools not to collect credits for them now, especially when the king needs oarsmen. They'll fetch a good price."

In the end, it was agreed to take them to Covehithe; none were to be killed. They might know of missing friends and relatives and could be questioned along the way.

At last. Catla checked the sun. It was past short-shadow time, so there was plenty of light yet for walking.

"Bring them here, Matthew," Hugh said. "Check their knots. We want no more escapes. We leave for Covehithe now. Those Norsemen will expect their comrades next day. We'll get there before that, late this night. The dark will hide us on the last part of the way. Let's use the light we have left now."

Edith called out, "Bring food. Fill your drinking horns and bring extra ones if you have them. There's water on the heath, but the ale is cleaner. At the signal, come back. Be quick."

Sven said, "On the way, Catla and I will tell you our plan. Catla only knows part of it because I haven't told her about getting into Covehithe using a way I know. We'll talk as we walk. We'll be at the standing stones while it's still light."

One older villager growled, "Who does he think he is? He can't tell us what to do."

In her mind, Catla agreed. Sven hadn't talked to her about any plan, and she felt annoyed. She had a plan of her own to use the path she'd taken the few times she'd ventured out after dark. The path was secret, known only to her family.

Hugh put his hand on Sven's shoulder and said, "Good idea, Sven."

Catla knew she'd have to speak up if her plan was to be heard, but now was not the time. Now was the time for leaving. They'd talk as they walked.

The prisoners arrived from the goat pen. Some villagers formed a guard. A rope looped around the first prisoner's neck was fastened to the neck of the man next in line, and so on, until all were secured together. Their hands were tied in front so they would have better balance. The hobbles around their legs were lengthened for faster walking.

One of them smiled and nodded at her. Did he think he knew her?

She looked more carefully. He nodded again.

Her head jerked back in annoyance. Who was he?

She flipped her hair and turned from him. *Late tonight, the dark will hide us.* Catla ran Hugh's words around in her head. She'd see her family tonight. Her spine tingled and her feet jigged a few small steps. She pushed worrisome thoughts away. She'd keep the image of them safe and well. For the first time in a long time, her smile started on the inside before it showed on her lips. "Thank you, thank you," she murmured, hoping some gods were listening.

CHAPTER TEN

Recrossing the heath

Catla pictured again the way she'd greet her family.
She'd cuddle Bega and rest her chin on her sister's soft
brown hair.

Clang!

Someone hit the iron hoop and the sound shattered
the image as she jumped, startled by the noise. Then
she imagined her father's voice teasing her. *Come on,
Catla, join the real world.*

"Thanks, Matthew," Hugh said. "That should bring
everyone. The prisoners look secure." Some Norsemen
stood with eyes lowered to avoid more jabs with the
staves. Others returned glare for glare, defiant even
in defeat.

A low voice growled in agreement. "Aye, they're secure all right and they don't appreciate our attention."

Catla peered into the crowd, wondering who was talking.

"Godrim always has something to say." A voice at her side supplied the answer to her unspoken question. She turned, delighted to see Edith.

"Look at them," Edith said to her. "They're a proud people, not used to being prisoners, except perhaps in war. It must hurt their pride to be captured by a bunch of villagers they expected to take easily as slaves."

"Are you suggesting we feel sorry for them?"

"No, Catla, no, of course not. I'm not sorry for them, not a bit. They brought this on themselves. It only reminds me that no one knows their own fate."

Catla gave herself a small shake to ease a sudden shiver.

"But then, you know that better than I do. Look at the way your life changed during a morning walk." Edith's hand clasped Catla's forearm in a light grip. "Forgive me. Am I upsetting you? Sometimes this old woman likes to muse."

"No. Besides, you're not old." Catla's mother talked like that sometimes, as if she saw things from a long way off, not caught right up in the middle of it. "Mother says things like that too. Father calls it fey time."

She pondered what that would be like, to be fey, to glimpse a world that is hidden from most folks. She hoped it would come to her. A chill puckered the skin on her arms, and she felt a pang of longing for her mother.

Edith voiced the words softly. "Fey time. I like that. I'll tell Hugh. I have much in common with your mother. I know you are anxious, Catla. Come, we'll join Sven so we can hear the new part of his plan." Before Catla could protest that she had a plan too, her hand was in Edith's. They scurried around the outskirts of the crowd to join Hugh. Edith's callused palm felt warm and firm against her own. The next time she had a chance to hold her mother's hand she would not shrug it off.

"We'll talk along the way," Hugh said, "and get our plan in place." Then he raised his voiced and called, "We're off. Covehithe before dawn."

Rufus, the blacksmith, shouted, "We'll show those barbarians that we Saxons know something about fighting too."

Catla cheered with the rest of the group, and then, in a surge, they set off. The villagers close to the prisoners brandished their staves, but the prisoners did not lag. Perhaps they were eager to get to Covehithe too.

Some people dodged their way to the front.

"Keep us in sight," Hugh called.

They waved, plunged over a small hillock and set off running toward a stand of elms.

"Are your legs tired, Catla? You've walked a long way this day." Sven moved to walk by her side.

"No, I'm fine." She smiled at him, warmed by his concern for her. "I'll be all right, but it is the farthest I've walked in one day. How about you? You were in York the day before we met. You've traveled even farther."

"I can cover a lot of distance in a day if I keep a steady pace. I'm used to it, but you're not."

The twist to his mouth and the way he emphasized *you're* made Catla glance at him sharply.

"It seems like a good pace," Sven said, "but we can slow down. For you too, Edith. We can slow right down for the two of you."

Catla shot Edith a questioning glance, and the twinkle in Edith's eyes confirmed that Sven was teasing. Sven turned his face, but Catla glimpsed his grin. Retaliating, she and Edith thumped his arms and shoulders, Catla trying to contain her giggles without success.

Sven turned back to face them, holding up his hands. Now he was laughing aloud. "All right, all right, stop now! I take it back. You are both very strong, fast walkers."

"Louder," Edith said. She reached up and grasped his ear between her thumb and forefinger and raised her voice to say, "Everyone needs to hear you."

"These two women are the fastest walkers in the world." Sven bellowed and some people turned to see what was causing the ruckus. Villagers smiled and shook their heads.

It had been a long time since Catla had laughed. She felt lightheaded and giddy.

"Did everybody hear that?" The volume of Edith's voice matched Sven's.

All around the group, villagers nodded and called back, "Yes!"

"Aye, Edith!"

"You're a fast walker, and so is Catla." Matthew chuckled as he said it.

When Edith seemed convinced Sven had suffered enough, she turned him loose and gave his ear a rub, then said so softly Catla almost didn't hear, "I hope I didn't hurt you."

"No, you were pretty gentle." Sven smiled at them. "I had it coming, and besides everyone needed a bit of a laugh, especially the two of you. You looked so serious."

"You two are ready for jesting at court," said Catla. Sven had been trying to relieve her low spirits, a side of him she had not seen before. "I know I've been gloomy," she added. "How do you stay lighthearted and optimistic? Aren't you worried about your father?"

"Yes, Sven," Edith said, "what about your father? You haven't talked about him."

"He wasn't in Covehithe when the Nord-devils came. He'd gone north a few days before the Norse fleet landed and sacked Scarborough. He's courting a woman who lives there, so he's frequently away from home these days. I don't know where he is now." Sven looked pensive.

"It's not good to keep all your worries to yourself. Talk if you want to," Catla said. "Remember the way you coaxed me to talk this morning."

"Thanks." Sven's smile was crooked. "He is all I have since Mother died. I pray that he is safe. I wish I knew where he was."

"I know how you feel," Catla said. "I hope he's all right." Sven's words sobered her, but she felt lighter after her laughter. She was on her way home. She turned and glanced back at the village.

With the dogs at the hill fort, Aigber was silent. It squatted in the warm sun. Not even a chicken scratched in the dirt. A sense of foreboding filled her mind. What would remain of Covehithe? It was harder and harder for her to imagine life continuing there, but she hoped Aigber would always be the peaceful place she'd first seen.

Her shadow stretched out in front, jostled by others of the same length. The sun would stay visible above the rim of the world for a long part of the walk. An occasional elm and oak tree towered over elder bushes. The air was soft and she felt calmer and happier than she had since she first saw Covehithe burn.

As she walked, she wondered how Olav was faring in the goat pen and if he was wearing that colorful coat he cared so much about, the one from Italia. That lovely cloth would not stand up well to goat droppings. Involuntarily, she giggled and was a little shocked at herself. Then she remembered her pledge to do what her parents wanted if they were safe. She would marry Olav. Her heart dropped at the idea, but Father said he was a good man, and Father was a good judge of character. It was the right thing to do, and Olav said he liked her and that he wanted to please her. She would try and reserve her opinions until she'd spent more time with him.

The villagers around the prisoners started calling out and boasting of what they would do to the Norsemen once they were in Covehithe.

"I'll run them through with my new short sword," Rufus said. "It's one of theirs. Serves them right."

"If there are any left, after I get there first," another voice answered.

Catla knew the first battle had been won through cunning and by avoiding any one-on-one fighting. But there would be no trap in Covehithe. They'd have to use swords and knives. Didn't these people understand the danger?

"Listen to you bragging. Everyone knows my sword will lead the way." As Matthew spoke, gales of catcalls erupted.

While listening to the talk, Catla burned with a sudden blaze of hatred for these Nord-devils. She thought it again: *Nord-devils*. There was no compassion in her even though Hugh had said, "No killing." She wished for enough nerve to use her stave to poke one of them hard enough to make him bleed. But she knew she could not do it. The thought of cutting into a man sickened her.

Dreadful visions of her family already slaughtered and the village empty and burned filled her mind. She panted as she struggled for control.

Edith's hand slipped into hers again and gave it a squeeze. "Warriors talk like that before going into danger. Don't be taken in by the light tones. There's trouble ahead, and we'll meet it. Keep your hopes up. We'll find them safe. The Norsemen there will be watching for the ship. They won't expect trouble, especially not from the heath."

Catla hugged Edith's arm close to her side. Edith gave Catla's hand a small pat and then she looked at Sven. "You say you have a plan?"

"Yes," said Sven. "I know a secret path."

"Enough secrets!" Catla exclaimed. "Where is your path? I know a path too. Maybe it's the same one."

Sven's eyebrows met in a frown, and then he raised them in surprise.

"What?" Catla said. "Do you think you're the only one who doesn't use the main path?"

"You've never mentioned it. I didn't know. Where does yours go?"

"My parents use it too. It's past the peat hut. Where does yours go?" she countered, startled at her demanding tone.

Sven looked at her and said, "It isn't exactly a secret. It comes down at the opposite end of the village from yours. You've likely seen it. It's steep. My father and I use it. I go to the standing stones mainly and look at the stars."

"The stars?" Catla's irritation eased as her interest sharpened.

Edith made a gesture with her hand as if asking Catla to listen and said, "Do you behold patterns in the heavens? Do you see them move with the seasons?" At his nod, she continued, "Do you feel a faint quaver to the air when you go into the circle of standing stones?" He nodded again. "Hugh and I have noticed these things. We don't know what it means, but something is different inside the circle."

"Yes," Sven said. Excitement made his voice higher and speech faster. "I thought I imagined it. You've felt it too? Did you watch the hairy-tailed star this spring?" But he didn't wait for a reply. "On the longest day, the sun, when it rises, shines directly on that big stone that lies along the eastern side of the circle. Have you noticed that?"

"Yes, we have. Have you said anything about this to anyone else?"

Sven shook his head. "No, I don't know what to make of it, so I stay quiet."

"Good idea. Be careful. Some people look for signs of evil in everything, or think the old religion is still kept."

"Yes," Sven said. His gaze seemed to turn inward for a moment. "But this has nothing to do with good or evil, old or new religions. It's just the sun on rocks and a weird feeling to the air. Now that Brother James has traveled farther north and Father John is here, people are less fearful, less anxious about evil."

"I like Father John better," Catla said, feeling excluded and anxious to join in.

"Brother James talked a lot about spirits and demons," Sven said. "He thought evil spirits caused milk to sour and that babies cried too long because devils were inside them and had to be cast out."

"Remember that baby who died when Brother James tried to shake the devils out?" Catla asked. "It was a few years ago so I don't remember whose baby it was. Was it Martha's? He said the devils were stuck and then when the baby was dead, he said she was better off because she was with God the Father and the devils would have taken her soul but she'd been released from their hold."

"I remember that," Sven said.

"Yes, so do I," said Edith. "We talked about it at the summer gathering that year. The women were so angry at the loss of an innocent. We agreed to help young mothers more so their babies wouldn't cry so long."

Catla caught sight of Hugh moving toward them. His tall form was easy to spot as he stopped and chatted with one group and then another.

"Here's Hugh coming now. Sven, he'll want to talk to you about these ideas, but they should wait until another time."

"Right. I'd like that."

"I look at the stars too," Catla said. "I don't go so far as the standing stones, like Sven, but I've gone up on the heath twice, and when I'm at the circle, the stones tell me stories." She had never told this to anyone. She looked anxiously at Edith and Sven, in case they laughed at her.

"Do you now?" Sven's tone of voice was thoughtful. "Do you see the patterns in the stars too, Catla?"

"I see groups of stars and I would like to see the patterns," she said.

"We will talk later," said Edith. "But now let's put our minds to defeating the Norsemen."

Hugh joined them and said, "Well, have you everything figured out? You've been talking so intently I'm sure a plan is in place." He turned aside and winked at Catla as he spoke.

"There's plenty of time before the standing stones, Hugh," Edith said. "Now you wouldn't be telling your good wife what to do?"

Catla's body stiffened. What would Hugh say? If she or her mother spoke like that to her father, there would be a swift and cutting tongue-lashing.

"Nay, nay, madam," Hugh said, chuckling as he spoke.

Catla was amazed at the friendly teasing in their voices. There was no anger. These two people laughed together. Would she ever find someone like that?

She had yet to laugh or even chuckle with Olav. She wasn't sure if he knew how to laugh. Her eyes lit on Sven. Was he more even in his temper? *Only sometimes*, she thought.

Hugh said, "Let's talk. We need to surprise the Norsemen. Sven, you have a plan?"

"I do," Sven said, "and so does Catla. She just told us she uses a hidden path too. The one I use is too dangerous, I think."

"Well, lad, the whole situation is dangerous. We need both a good plan and some good luck. Catla, what about yours?"

"Mine has danger with it too. It comes into the village close to the goat pen."

"That's where the villagers are, isn't it?" Hugh pondered this news as Hindley and Matthew joined them.

"Sven, where does your path enter the village?" Edith asked.

"Opposite end to Catla's. Closer to the council fire," said Sven.

"We plan to free the Covehithe prisoners before we attack the Norsemen," Matthew said. "They are known to sleep at council rings. If we use your path, Sven, they will be between the Covehithe prisoners and us. That's not good."

"Yes," Sven replied. "It's not an easy path and in the wrong location. What's the danger in using your path, Catla? I didn't know there was a path there."

"We use it sometimes to go up on the heath," Catla said. "It's narrow and goes up through some bushes, around a big boulder and then ends at the top in the middle of some bracken. We go a slightly different way each time so we don't make a visible track. It's steeper than the main pathway."

"The bracken is a problem," Hugh said. "It's noisy. The Norsemen could hear us."

"What's your solution to that, Catla?" asked Edith.

"We'll have to go one-by-one, slowly, and hold the bracken fronds so they don't hit each other. Bracken is only at the top and for a short way down the hill before the bushes take over."

"It'll take too long," Hindley protested. "They'll hear us. What's at the bottom?"

"Yes, it will take longer," said Catla. "But they won't hear us if we're careful. At the bottom there's a clearing within the bushes. The winter peat storage hut is beyond the bushes. It's open on all sides but almost full. We can hide behind it and be close to the goat pen. The Nord—Norsemen, won't know about the path."

"Catla's right," Sven said. "The shed is almost full and no one pays any attention to the bushes beyond.

It is the best way into Covehithe. We'll come out very close to the prisoners."

"How far is it from the goat pen to the peat hut?" Matthew said.

"Only about three oars' lengths," Sven replied. "Do you agree, Catla?"

At her nod, Hugh said, "This sounds like our best plan. Better than passing the Norsemen before we free the prisoners. What do you all think?"

"It's far enough away from the council fire that the Norsemen won't hear," Sven added.

"I agree," Matthew said.

"Then it's settled," Hugh said. The talk became more general. Catla was excited. Her plan was a good one, and Hugh had listened. Maybe she would talk to her father about Olav and the things that were bothering her about him. Maybe he'd listen too.

She looked around for landmarks to tell how far they'd come. Aigber was no longer in sight. They'd passed the Elder Bush Hill some way back, so she knew they were getting close to the standing stones. Some distance ahead was a stand of oaks like those beside the stones. Her long shadow bobbed across the headland. The dips and mounds were like dark pouches and the bushes looked dusky on their shadow sides. The sun was more than halfway down the sky, but it warmed her back.

"We've covered a good distance," said Hugh. "The moon is over half full, and it's rising late. Its light will help us. Our night vision will get better as it gets darker. The Norsemen will have been standing guard, looking into campfires."

Catla remembered how thick and black the night seemed when she turned away from the council fire. At first everything was black, like soot-shadows under the ridgepole of her cottage. Then gradually she'd see the shape of things again.

"Aye," said Hindley. "The captains always said to look beyond the fire or stand with our backs to it on guard duty, although usually we looked at the flames. And we couldn't see into the night. They'll do the same. They underestimate us and won't be worried. The night will be dark enough to protect us."

"What if there's a sentry on top of the hill to watch the heath?" asked Catla.

"They'll not bother," Hugh said. "They won't expect trouble from this direction. I doubt they'll expect trouble at all, but we'll send a scout to check. Good idea, Catla."

"You're right," Matthew said. "We're the only two villages along this piece of land. They're used to controlling small places like ours."

"They'll look to the sea for the ship," said Edith, "and won't expect it until the morrow. We'll surprise them this night."

This night. The words seemed to echo, and Catla was startled to realize this was only her second night away from home. Last night she'd slept alone in the standing stones. So much had happened, the time seemed longer.

By now, other villagers crowded in to listen and offer opinions. Ideas flew around like starlings, so fast Catla couldn't keep track of who was saying what.

One voice was loud and clear. "I'm not sure that bracken path will work."

"We should gather on top of the hill that overlooks the village, and at the signal, we'll rush them."

"No, that would get some of us killed, for sure. Why don't we…?"

"The sea. Go down to the sea and around over the beach and rocks, and come up…"

"That might work, but aren't the…?"

"No, it'd take too long. And anyway, how do you get down to the water before the village? We haven't got…"

"Enough, enough." Hugh's voice held a command.

Edith sounded exasperated. "We'll follow Catla's path. Listen to the girl! She may be young, but she knows what she is talking about."

"Now, now, don't fret yourself, Edith," Hindley said.

Hugh cut off further discussion. "We're going to use Catla's idea." He asked her to go over the plan again, and this time she felt more confident. There weren't any objections when she was finished. A few people patted her on the back.

"I agree that Catla's plan is sound, but what if a few of us who know about nets go around by the cove and gather their nets to use like we did at Aigber?" Matthew asked. "Catla, do the fishermen leave their nets by the shoreline?"

Catla nodded.

"Yes," Hugh said, after a pause while he considered the idea. "Good thinking, Matthew. Get a small group and plan it. Come at them from the cove side. Anyone else have another idea?"

"What about a few of us using Sven's path to make sure none of them escape over the heath?" Rufus, the smith, asked.

"Good. We'll discuss any changes at the standing stones," Hugh said. "Now, go and talk it over with everyone, especially the guards. Everyone should know the exact location of the peat hut, the goat pen, the clearing and the path."

"If you think of anything, we need to hear about it now before we begin," Edith said. "Don't keep your worries, fears or ideas to yourself. We have one chance to make this work. Everyone is part of it."

"One thing has occurred to me," Catla said. "When we reach the standing stones, we should gag our prisoners so they don't yell warnings."

"That's the idea. This is what I mean," Edith said. "Speak out if something occurs to you. It doesn't matter if others have thought it, saying it out loud helps us think of everything."

"Catla, thank you," Hugh said. "We'll see to that. Matthew, do you have wadding and extra lengths of leather thongs?"

At Matthew's nod, Hugh waved his arm in dismissal. "Aye. You know what to do. Make sure everyone understands what will happen when we arrive in Covehithe."

Some people's eyes grew wide and wary, while other folks narrowed theirs to slits, but everyone seemed satisfied. They knew the dark would help them by hiding their movements, but Catla wondered if anyone dreaded being out of their cottages at night. Did they fear the unseen like some of the people in her village did? Catla had felt that fear last night. Thinking about her mother had helped her sleep, finally. This night many people would keep each other safe. Would she hear the wolves howl under the roof of the stars in a plaintive chorus? This would be her family's second night in the goat pen. Would they post their own watch? Would the women rub themselves with goat's turds so they were repellent to the Nord-devils?

Mother had told her stories of famous women warriors like Queen Boudicca, who had won battles against the Roman centurions. Mother said it gave her courage when she went into battle, to know other women had done the same thing. Aethelflaed, Queen of Mercia, had led her army to battle and won. Mercia lay some miles to the south of them on the other side of the River Humber, but close enough that Mother felt connected. Thinking about those brave women now gave Catla courage. Mother and Father would be doing everything in their power to keep the family and villagers safe. Surely the slave-raiders would keep them whole and strong. Oh, if only she knew for sure. Her heart pounded again, and she tasted bile. Tears threatened to gush until she shook her shoulders. *Do not give in to these evil fears. No one is aided by them*, she told herself. She turned her fear to anger and let it move her forward.

CHAPTER ELEVEN

A Startling Discovery

People talked over the plan so everyone would know exactly what to do each step of the way. Catla looked for someone to talk with, but saw only groups of older men. She supposed they would prefer to hear the details from their friends, so she walked alone with her own thoughts and gradually her anger subsided. Her chest expanded with hope as she breathed in the evening air. It felt good. She was on her way home! And they had a fine plan.

After a few more steps, she frowned as doubts came tumbling in. They didn't have a trap. They'd fight on level ground, face to face. Images of the marauders flooded in and swept her hope away. Then she recalled her father's words about holding an image in her mind. Resolutely, she created a picture, detail upon detail, of her family greeting each other: Bega's brown eyes; Cuthbert's hair, even curlier than hers; her mother's warm smile; and Stoutheart's big doggie grin.

Edith had reminded her that no one knows their own fate. When Catla had gone to the heath the day before, she hadn't known what that would mean for her village. What if she hadn't left the hill when she did? She might not have been as far as the standing stones and Sven might have missed seeing her. The idea startled her. This day would be different. He'd helped her tell her story in Aigber. He'd stopped her from running into the Norsemen by Elder Bush Hill. Without him, she could be on a slave ship instead of walking back to Covehithe.

Looking around, she saw two or three groups of Aigber folks talking to the prisoners. Every family had relatives or knew of someone stolen in earlier slave raids. They were trying to find out if those people were still alive and where they were.

Hugh had told the villagers that if they wanted to talk to the prisoners it had to be while they were walking to the standing stones; after that, the prisoners would be gagged. Even so, people kept a fair distance, and the prisoners' hands were bound so they could do no harm.

Loud voices and a sudden scuffle interrupted her thoughts.

Anson, Rufus's son, strode beside a prisoner who had blood running down his face. "Why should we let these men live?" he yelled. "This swine had a knife and was cutting at his wrist straps. I got it away and knocked him one on the nose."

Hugh strode to his side and said, "You didn't hurt him much. He won't slow us down. Good man, Anson." He patted him lightly on the shoulder. "Now, you've got a new knife. It's a nice one too. We'd try to escape, too, in their position." He raised his voice and called loudly, "Stay alert, everyone. Double your watch on the prisoners. Those of you questioning the prisoners, keep a good distance."

Catla lagged a bit to walk beside Anson. He was pleased with himself and gave the man a quick jab in the ribs with the knife hilt. She said, "Is it as good a knife as Hugh says, Anson?"

"Yes, it's got a different piece of metal forged into it." He raised it to show her the dark twisted vein running along the shaft of the blade.

"That gives the blade extra strength. It is fine," she said. "My mother's short stabbing sword has the same look."

"Even better. Everyone knows Sarah has good weapons. This one is mine now." He tucked it into the leather belt that secured his shift. "Do you know the plan?"

She told him in detail and ended by asking, "What do you think?"

"That should work. It's better than charging over the hill yelling like banshees."

"I agree, Anson, but I..."

"You agree with this fellow? Don't listen to him. He's never right." Chad came up behind them. "He makes things up to impress pretty girls. Especially those with red hair."

"My hair is not red, not really!" Catla blurted the words and then blushed at her fib and that he'd called her pretty.

Chad jostled against her and said, "I suppose you don't have freckles either?"

"At least I'm not pigeon-toed," she said. Her face flamed as she turned and stormed off, her hair swinging behind her. She tried to close her ears to Chad's teasing voice when he called after her, "It looks like it's on fire in the sun, Catla. Are you sure it's not red?"

She picked up speed, and when she was almost at the head of the line of prisoners, she heard her name whispered. She glanced sharply at an older prisoner who held her gaze. He was the one who had nodded to her back in Aigber when the prisoners arrived from the goat pen. Then softly, he spoke again. "Catla."

"Do you know me? Do I know you?" she asked.

"I've been to your village and bought your mother's beer," he said in English.

"So, it was you who brought the raid to us!" She was furious.

"Not so. I promise you. But listen. There's something you need to know," he said.

Catla was interested but alarmed at the same time. "You know my mother and father? Where did you learn our language?"

"From our slave, when I was a boy."

"You had a slave! To live as a slave is a wasted life. That's what I think of slavery!" She stamped her foot as she spoke.

"Ah, but isn't that what will happen to us prisoners?" he asked.

"Yes, it is." Catla hated to agree, but he was right.

"What you mean is, you don't believe in slavery if your people are the slaves, but it's all right if other peoples are slaves?"

Catla didn't know how to answer. She felt confused but chastened. That *was* the way she thought.

"That topic is for a later day. Keep your voice low. I don't want my companions to overhear. The fellows in front and back of me don't speak your language but others do." The words hissed out of him. "I have something important to tell you. Act bored. The others will think I'm just talking to a pretty girl. Nod once in a while to let me know you are hearing me."

"Why should I? Who are you to tell me what to do?"

"As I said, I have important news for these people. That is, if they care about keeping their lives."

"All right, tell me fast."

"I will, but first, there's something for you to consider. If I help you, will you try and convince your father to let me join one of your villages?"

"Join a village? Are you mad?"

"I have some wealth. I'm too old for this Viking way of life. I want to settle someplace. Be a farmer."

"A farmer?" Catla laughed as she appraised him. He was stocky, with powerful arms and shoulders. His face was half hidden by a beard. His eyes were blue and clear as the skies. "Who are you?"

"Ragnar," he replied. "I'm a lord's son, but younger sons don't inherit land. We go raiding and trading instead."

"What is it you've got to tell me? Be quick. Maybe I'll help you. What's so important?"

"Another ship is coming to Covehithe. Its crew is to have first choice of you. You are all to be slaves."

"We've beaten you once and we can do it again."

"Nay, Catla. That's foolish pride talking. There's something you don't know. The new ship belongs to the king's commander, Helgi. His crew is tougher than this pathetic group and there are more of them. Our group was supposed to capture everyone in both villages. They want everybody."

At his words, Catla's head jerked up and she looked right at him. "Do you think anyone has died?"

"It's hard to say. These are slow-witted men, some of them. All I know is that Helgi wants everyone. The men are afraid of the commander. They do what he tells them. Get this information to Hugh. Your people need to know it. I'll talk to him. I can speak for myself."

With a quick backward glance, Catla hurried past the rest of the prisoners.

Ragnar. She repeated his name so she'd remember.

Where was Hugh?

A new ship.

Helgi.

What would that do to the plan?

Her heart quickened. Was this a trap? The new ship might be in the cove already. Is that why the prisoners had seemed ready to make the trek? Could Ragnar be trusted?

She needed to find Hugh. She hurried forward and spotted the standing stones. She'd never come at them from this direction and they looked different. She was halfway home. She longed for her parents' warm arms and Bega's smiles. Soon she'd see them. Soon. She pushed down the voice that warned her not to be too sure. What if the other ship was there already? She thrust that thought aside.

Where was Hugh?

CHAPTER TWELVE

A Rest at the Standing Stones

People straggled into the circle of standing stones, but Catla didn't see Hugh among them. She pressed both hands against her breastbone to slow her heart and stepped past the long entrance stone. The purple flowers that grew along its easterly side were going to seed. Standing still for a moment, she sent a silent hello to the stones, her old friends. She imagined their low greetings rumbling back to her. Odin stood to her left. At her right was Thor. Her fingers traced the rough-hewn surfaces, plucked at mossy crevices and trailed over planes and angles. She looked for the stone she called Mars, standing a bit aloof, as if he couldn't mix with the rest of them. The thought made her smile.

As she moved closer to the center, she remembered Sven telling Edith he noticed a difference in the air when he was inside the circle. She paused to sense if she could feel anything. She didn't.

Her legs were tired, and the sore one pulsed. She struggled to keep her balance on the uneven ground. The belt holding her pouch, knife and drinking horn had loosened; she pulled it close again and tucked in the leather ends. Running her hand across her shift she wondered if it could ever be clean again. Across the circle, Hugh sat with his back against Ravensclaw, the large stone across from the opening. She moved toward him, stepping around resting villagers, nodding greetings. The boys and men who sat surrounding Hugh took no notice of her, but Ragnar's words urged her on. "Hugh," she said. "Hugh, I need to tell you something."

He turned and beckoned to her with his raised arm. "Come. Sit here, Catla."

A few men grumbled.

"Make room for the girl, you big oafs," Matthew chided them. Catla glanced up at him, surprised by his help. The men shifted to make a small space. She squeezed into it and stretched her legs out along the ground.

When she was settled, Hugh said, "Are you comfortable?"

She nodded.

"What's bothering you?"

"I was talking to one of the prisoners, or rather he was talking to me." Hugh's eyebrows rose and a couple of the men snickered.

Her cheeks burned, but she stayed quiet. Hugh frowned at them and said sternly, "All right. Let her speak." He patted Catla's shoulder. "What did he say?"

"Ragnar—his name's Ragnar—learned English from a slave when he was a boy, but that's not the most important thing he said."

"Go on," Hugh said.

"He wants to talk to you, Hugh. He said another ship's coming to Covehithe with the commander of all their king's ships."

"Helgi." The name burst from Hugh's mouth.

"Yes, that's what Ragnar called him," Catla said.

"You know of him?" Hindley asked Hugh, interrupting Catla.

"By reputation," Hugh said. "He's a fierce fighter. This is important but grave news. I wonder how he's connected to our prisoners? Anything else, Catla?"

"When it arrives," Catla said, "the commander is to have first choice from all the people in our villages for the slave market."

Another buzz of voices erupted. "Slave market! As we thought."

"I've heard of Helgi too, Hugh," Matthew said.

"When is he coming?" Hindley asked. "Where's his ship now? Is it already there?"

Voices merged into each other.

"Quiet! Quiet!" Hugh snapped. Catla jumped a bit. Folks farther away turned to listen.

"What's going on? What is it?" People crowded closer.

"We've learned something new," Hugh said. "Well done, my girl!" Hugh ruffled her hair and gave her shoulders a short hug.

Edith entered the circle and moved toward them.

"Gather here, everyone," Hugh called. After Edith had slipped in beside Catla, he continued. "One of the prisoners spoke to Catla. We must think about this carefully. The prisoner Ragnar claims to have information about Covehithe."

As Hugh spoke, Catla saw the prisoners arrive. They sat well outside the circle of stones. The guards stooped, moving from man to man, checking their bindings.

Hugh repeated what Catla had told him. A few people said, "Helgi," as if they knew of him. Hugh said, "This night's fight will be more dangerous than we thought if Helgi's ship is there." Turning to Catla, he said, "Tell them about the slaving." He pushed her into standing.

"Ragnar told me they were after slaves," she said. Her eyes sought Sven's, whose head jerked up. He looked her fully in the face for a moment. "Maybe they won't kill anyone if they want them all for slaves."

"That's good news!" Edith reached for Catla's hand.

Catla felt comforted to know Edith's concern for the people of Covehithe almost matched her own.

"Don't be too hasty to make a leap in that direction," Hindley said. "Some of these men consider it a sport to kill the ones they think won't bring a good price. Saves having to feed them."

Catla's legs suddenly gave out and she sat with a thump.

"Hindley!" Edith's tone was sharp and full of reprimand. She put a protective arm around Catla's shoulders. "Think who you're talking to. Catla and Sven don't need any more dire warnings than what they already carry in their own heads."

The people around Hindley poked him and frowned. He looked chastened and said, "Sorry, Catla and Sven. My mouth runs away sometimes."

"Did he say when the ship would come?" Matthew asked, bringing the talk back to Helgi.

"No." Catla gulped. She blinked in shock over Hindley's words, and she felt sick again. "Let me think. No, he just said it is coming."

All eyes shifted back to Hugh, who patted Catla's knee. "Helgi is a fearless warrior and he's trained his men to be the same. Let's hope we arrive at Covehithe first. I may know more after I speak to Ragnar."

"What if the ship's already in Covehithe, Hugh?" Edith asked.

"That will prove difficult," Hugh said.

Catla had wanted to ask the same question, but she'd dared not inside this circle. Catla had learned many myths from Old Ingrid, who believed ancient gods had been worshipped in stone circles. Catla wasn't convinced. But Old Ingrid had impressed on her that the gods were mischief-makers, interfering in peoples' lives just for the impish fun of it. Now, Catla hoped they weren't listening. No one needed more vexing. The gods were best left undisturbed.

"Should we change our plan, Hugh?" Hindley asked.

"No. We've considered everything. Catla's path is best, no matter how many Norsemen are in the village. The group using Sven's path will block that way, and they'll watch the council fire but won't move until they see our group advancing. Rest now until Theodore arrives from the hill fort. We're in for a much bigger fight if Helgi's ship is there before us."

A *bigger fight*. The words were ominous. Catla's hands were clenched into tight fists. Slowly, she released the tension and flexed her fingers.

"We're basing a lot on the word of an enemy," Matthew said. "How can we trust him? What if he lies?"

"Let's not take a chance. Let's tie him up and leave him here," Hindley said. "When the attack's over, we'll come back and get him if the wolves haven't got him first."

Catla shuddered at the gruesome thought.

"We could do that, Hindley," Hugh said. "Whatever we agree, I am going to talk to him. He could have kept quiet. We'd never have known about Helgi. What purpose does it serve him to have spoken? If he wanted to work against us, he'd have said nothing." Then he said, "Catla, let's find Ragnar."

Catla's shift and apron felt heavy. It was hard to lift her knees against them as she hurried after Hugh toward the prisoners. Some burrs of seedpods were stuck to the tan wool of her shift and they rubbed at her ankles. Her legs were tired and stiff and she knew she limped, but she was curious. She believed Ragnar had told the truth. She sensed no harm toward her in him. He said he'd drunk her mother's beer.

But that hardly seemed enough to earn her trust. *Don't be a gull, my girl,* she told herself. She smiled as she echoed the words her mother had said to her at the fair in York.

As they neared the prisoners, some of them shouted rough-sounding words while others sat with their heads down. "Water, they're asking for water," Hugh said. "Rufus, go and ask if anyone has extra water or beer. Even if it's a mouthful. Tell them to bring it here. Be careful giving it to them."

"There he is, Hugh. There's Ragnar." Catla pointed out the man, and Hugh moved closer to him. Some of the prisoners shot evil looks at their comrade, but Hugh snapped out a few Norse words and they turned their eyes away. They could do nothing. Hugh untied the rope around Ragnar's neck, retied it to the next prisoner in line and led Ragnar from the group.

When Hugh gestured, Catla spoke. "Ragnar, this is Hugh, the headman of Aigber. I told him what you said."

Ragnar was shorter than Hugh. His hair was lighter than Catla's but also red. Like most of the village men, he wore it tied back.

He looked at Hugh and said, "I wish you no harm. I would like to help."

"You're in a difficult position here," Hugh said with a glance at the prisoners. "Still, I'm surprised you want to help us." Then he turned to Catla and said, "I'll see how far this change of heart goes. He's tied and shackled. I'll talk with him but keep my knife close to hand."

Ragnar glanced at Hugh but stayed silent. Catla wondered what he'd say to help Hugh make up his mind.

"Catla, ask Matthew and Hindley to come. We'll talk to this fellow together. You need to find a place to lie down and sleep. You're tired. I promised Edith I'd keep my eye on you."

"All right, Hugh." She found Hindley and Matthew and delivered Hugh's message. The prisoners had been gagged by the time she passed them again. She glanced back at Hugh and Ragnar. Hugh nodded once or twice. Ragnar was doing most of the talking. She was curious, but her legs needed rest, especially her sore one.

The same spot where she'd slept last night by Odin's stone was sunny. She settled in and felt herself relax. Last night Sven had found her here. Now, all of Aigber was on the march. They were midway home. They'd arrive tonight. Dread and anticipation swirled in her head.

As she settled down, Theodore, Brida and the girls arrived from the hill fort, and Catla listened to a wave of talk and questions. She was envious as she watched them greet their fathers. Her arms longed for her family. She turned aside to hide her yearning.

Sven walked across the circle and threw his long body down beside hers. He nudged a bit closer and put his hand on her arm. He said, "Don't be impatient, Red."

"Red!"

"I call you that when I think of you."

"But my hair isn't...You think of me?"

"Do you mind?"

"Well." She hesitated. The little boys called her Red when she shooed the foxes away from their traps. *Red, Red, the fox's guard. Sticks her head in the midden yard.* But she was intrigued with the idea of Sven thinking about her. "I don't hate it when you say it, but..."

"Leave it for now," Sven said. "Besides, since you're betrothed, I shouldn't even be talking to you. I'll move if you want."

Catla answered, "No, I don't want you to move. And anyway, I'm not betrothed, not quite. Aren't we friends?"

"I guess, for now."

"For now?" Catla asked.

"What about Olav? I don't like him. I don't think you should marry him. He won't make you happy. And then there's the way you were flirting with Anson earlier. *Oh, Anson, what a beautiful knife.* It was sickening."

"It was?" Catla's heart bumped hard against her ribs. "You don't like Olav, you don't like Anson and, apparently, you don't like me! Why are you here then? To upset me?"

"Oh, by the raven's bill, I've done it again," Sven said. "I've put both of my feet into my mouth at the same time."

His face—downcast eyes and cheeks flaming red—looked comical. Catla was tempted to laugh, but she wanted more answers, so she said, "Why don't you like Olav?"

"All he ever talks about is himself," Sven said. "Haven't you noticed? No matter what other people are talking about, he manages to turn it around to his travels and how well he is doing as a peddler."

"Maybe you're jealous." As she said the words, Catla was surprised at her boldness and waited to hear what he'd say.

"No, I'm not. Well, maybe I am, a little, because I don't think he'll be right for you. What I say is true. Haven't you noticed that?"

"Yes, yes, I have," she said. "I tried not to pay attention to it, because Mother says I have to respect older people. But he never listens to anything I say. I thought he was nervous and ignoring me made him feel important."

"I suppose. But he does it no matter who's there. Even with people like your father, who already thinks Olav's a fine fellow."

"My father does like him, doesn't he? He doesn't usually like that kind of person."

"In any case, will people talk if I lie here?"

"I don't know, maybe. Do you care? Will you think less of me if I agree to let you lie beside me?"

"Why, no, that is, no…"

"Then why did you say it?" Catla was cross now and pushed him away. She turned her back to him and closed her eyes. She would try to sleep. That would fix him! But try as she might, she could not slip into sleep. Sven's last words played in her ears, but she felt too cross to talk. All around them people chattered and laughed. Soon Sven's easy breathing told her he slept and that made her even more cross.

Hugh came back and brought Ragnar into the circle. He held his arms high, signaling for quiet. "Ragnar thinks Helgi expects his other ship to need time in Aigber to capture us and loot the village. They'd likely wait for the next outgoing tide, and you can be sure they'll know the tides. They won't feel in any hurry and so won't navigate against that current at night when the ship's fully loaded with villagers. He will expect them to be back on the morrow. He'll likely come then too."

His news was greeted by a buzz of talk, but it seemed to Catla that most people had figured this out already.

"Rest for a little while before we start out." Hugh continued to speak. "We have about the same distance to walk as we've covered. We'll start out with some light."

When Hugh said "start out," Catla wanted to shout, *Hurry up!* She knew it was unreasonable, but she sat up and shifted her legs as if getting ready to go again.

Sven stirred and whispered, "Be patient, Catla. We need their help. It's better if everyone rests. You need rest too. We have time."

People lay on the ground or sat propped against the stones. Catla knew Sven was right. She released the lip she'd bitten to stop from arguing. She let herself sink back down to the sandy earth, and she fell into a light sleep. She awakened to Sven's hand rubbing her arm gently. "It's time, Catla. We're getting ready."

"Catla and Sven, you lead," Hugh said. "Everyone— keep your voices low. We won't be heard from here, but we'll be used to speaking softly. We'll rest again, when it's closer to sunup. Then we'll move into Covehithe with the predawn light."

It was evening now and the light was fading. The last part of the journey would be tricky in the dark.

Catla's legs felt less tired. A pleasant jolt of excitement tingled under her ribs.

Hugh raised his voice. "Get used to walking silently. We make a lot of noise when we move. It will be a still night and noise travels far. We must not alert our enemy."

Catla walked with Sven, followed by Brida and Theodore's group. Hugh walked beside Ragnar, and a group of men followed right behind them, their hands on the hilts of their knives. The prisoners shuffled along without protest. New energy surged in the air. Catla lifted her gaze. Stars were beginning to show in the northeastern sky, in the direction they were heading. She looked for a bright one to wish on. Besides thinking of her family's safety, she was mulling about Sven. He was jealous of Olav. She smiled.

Twilight lingered long during the harvest part of the year. It remained after the sun disappeared below the earth's rim. Bright fingers of light pierced upward into the blue-gray clouds. The colors darkened into peach and mauve and purple as the light died. Catla looked back toward Aigber. The stones stood dark against the magnificent sky. Ahead, the heavens darkened.

CHAPTER THIRTEEN

In the Dark

With the evening light, the path was clearly visible. Catla was surprised, since it had been hard to see last evening when she was alone. After a while, a fainter path veered off to the right. Was this the one to follow? "Have you been on this path, Sven?" she asked as she slowed.

"No, but it goes in the right direction, toward your end of the village."

"We'll take it." She turned onto it. "Thank Our Lady, we are getting closer. My legs are tired."

"Well, you've walked a lot in these last two days."

"Was it farther than to Scarborough or York?" Catla asked. "This year we sold Mother's wool at both fairs."

"Did you rest on the way to the fairs?"

"Sometimes."

"Long enough to feel refreshed?"

"Yes. We didn't hurry. And we slept by the road on both journeys. Father said the fairs would wait for us. Buyers like Mother's purple wool. She sells all she makes."

"Your mother's colors are famous along this coast. Is she teaching you her secrets?"

"Yes." Catla felt a guilty blush, remembering how she often slipped away from the dye pots. She was proud of her mother's skill and liked what the money her mother earned could buy: seeds, tools, salt and sometimes a piece of soft linen for a shift under her smock. *I will do better*, she vowed silently.

"I'm tired too, Catla." Sven glanced at her. "It's still a long way." He looked at her more closely. "Are you limping?"

"Only a little."

"What's the matter?"

She lifted one side of her skirt and showed him the way her leg was bruised from her fall. He gasped and called out softly, "Edith, come and look at this."

Catla wished she had masked her limp better. Edith moved up and looked at her leg.

"When did you do this, Catla? Last day?"

Catla hesitated.

"You're being too brave. It should have had a poultice on it. Does it hurt?"

"A little, just now."

"You are a true hero, my girl. You don't like fuss, do you?"

Catla shook her head, and Edith gave her a quick hug. "We can do nothing now, but we could rest here."

Catla squeezed Edith's hand in gratitude. "No, it's almost dark. Let's go. There's still light. We'll rest later and wait for the moon to rise."

Hugh walked up to them and said, "We should keep going. Is everything all right?"

"We were looking at the ugly bruise Catla has on her leg," Edith said.

"I'm fine," said Catla. "Hugh is right. Let's move. We can talk as we go."

"Good," said Hugh. "Ragnar is with Matthew and Hindley. He says there are about the same number of Norsemen in the village as we have already captured. That will be another twenty. The ship was not full. Many of their warriors died at Stamford Bridge. They were counting on slaves at the oars to take it home. We'll have an easier time than we thought if Helgi's ship hasn't arrived. There are only about forty in the whole crew."

"Forty," said Catla, and she flashed fingers on both hands as she counted.

Hugh said, "Ragnar told me this crew is made up of men cast off from other crews."

"Cast off?" Catla hadn't heard that term before.

"Men other crews wanted to get rid of because they weren't good fighters or stirred up trouble with crew members, that sort of thing."

"But, Hugh," Catla said, "Ragnar doesn't seem like that."

"No. He's part of the group because of a family feud between his family and Helgi's. The king promised to name Ragnar the commander of his ships, but his father could not raise as many men for the battle as Helgi's father, so the king gave the command to Helgi. Ragnar thinks Helgi wants to kill him, to rid himself of a rival, especially now that their king is dead. None of Ragnar's people know where he is right now, so if he's dead…" Hugh shrugged and didn't need to complete the thought.

"Why did Ragnar agree to come with that crew of men if they're so useless?" asked Sven.

"Back in his land, he was knocked senseless by Helgi's men, then carried onto one of his ships," said Hugh. "When he came to, they were at our shores."

"His life is in danger, no matter what he does," Catla said.

"Seems so," Hugh said. "That's why he spoke up. He'd like a chance for a decent life in one of our villages."

"Will he help us fight?" Sven asked.

"He's a good fighter, but none of our people will like the idea of giving him a sword."

"He's canny, isn't he, Hugh?' Catla said.

"Yes, he is. He's also plainspoken and perceptive. I like that. But we'll keep an eye on him, no matter. Are we getting close, Catla?"

"There's a shorter hill before we get to the hill-crest that overlooks the village. We'll stop this side of it," she said. "We'll be far enough away to whisper while we rest."

"Anson said he'd scout the heath when we get a little closer," Hugh said. "He's fast and wary. Catla, can you find the way in the dark?"

"I think so. There weren't that many paths. I haven't been this far on the heath at night, but I know it well by day. Besides, the moon is almost full. When it rises, the light will help."

"You'll find the way," Edith said.

"We'll leave the prisoners behind where we stop," Hugh said. "They're gagged and tied. A couple of folks have said they'll stay as guards."

"We should slow down now," Edith said. "The shadows are tricky and the moon rises late."

Catla thought about Ragnar as she tromped along. His life was far different from anything she knew.

She'd met traders who came to their village, but no one had talked to her like he had. He was like a slave to his own people. No wonder he wanted to get away. He was younger than Olav. Would Ragnar come to live in Covehithe? The evening council meetings would be interesting with all the tales he must have. Would he like village life? Or would he be lonesome? Maybe he'd want to marry. Martha had two young sons and had been lonesome since Uhtred died two summers ago. Maybe they'd like each other.

Catla was startled to realize she was thinking about life after the rescue. Her heart quickened and it became easier to put one foot in front of the other. Her mind was lulled by the rhythm of her footsteps, but she kept a good hold on her thoughts and would not let them roam into thinking about her family. She vowed again to be a better daughter, kinder and more willing to do her work without being asked. In this brief time apart she'd realized how much her mother and her whole family meant to her.

"Now the moon is rising. See it over the water?" Edith took Catla's arm and turned her in the direction of the sea. A lopsided oval disc was rising from the horizon, casting a path of shimmering gray light across the dark water. Catla sighed with gratitude. She was back to her land and her sea.

Then she smelled smoke. She plucked at Edith's sleeve and whispered, "Do you smell it?" They stopped and people bumped into each other because their eyes had been following their feet, not looking ahead. Hugh moved beside them, and Catla whispered, "There's smoke." He nodded.

"We're close enough, even though smoke drifts a long way." Catla spoke quietly. "The short hill rises just ahead. We'll rest here."

"Now would be a good time to rub dirt into our faces and hands," Sven said.

"Right," Hugh said. "We'll stop until the moon shifts farther west, and then move for the attack just before dawn." Then he said to Anson, "This is a good time to go. Check for any lookouts. Do you want to rest first?"

"No. I'll be back directly." He slipped into the dark.

Catla sank to the ground. Heather cushioned her back and she leaned against it, her eyes wide at first. The moon rose higher in the sky. It looked like the Roman coin she had wrapped in a scrap of tanned leather and tucked beneath her sleeping robe in her cottage. Would it still be there? She'd found it on the heath and her parents let her keep it, a dowry for the future. She thought it brought good luck, even though Father John did not approve of placing faith in objects unless they came from a pilgrimage. Only religious icons held power for good, he said. Still, she imagined her golden coin up in the sky, leading and protecting them.

She dozed and then wakened with small starts and dozed again. The moon was taking forever to cross that little space of sky. She had drunk all her ale, and eaten the chunk of bread and hard cheese Edith had put into the leather pouch that hung from her belt.

In the moonlight she saw groups of people standing and moving about. Then her eyes would close and she'd wake feeling anxious that she'd slept too long, only to see people still at rest. Anson had returned some while ago to report he'd seen no guards.

"The moon is right. Time to move, Catla," Hugh whispered. There were fewer people now. The fishermen had gone. They'd be making their way along the shore and would come into the village after they'd gathered the Covehithe fishing nets on the way. The group that was using Sven's path had gone. Now the remaining people shuffled into a single line behind her, Sven at her back. Fighting partners stood next to each other. They would cross the short hill, then climb the last one with the bracken at the start of the hidden path. Catla's stomach flipped with fear and excitement, the calm displaced. Would she find the right path, the one that led to her family and the Nord-devils?

CHAPTER FOURTEEN

The Wolf's howl

The moon hovered at the peak of the heavens, before edging toward the western horizon. It was the deepest part of the night, but other concerns pushed worries about goblins aside as Catla moved along the path to Covehithe. She stopped and looked out over the water. Infinite ripples glimmered across waves. The sea. She was home.

The far eastern rim of the ocean melted into the sky with a first gray hint of dawn. Turning back, she faced the bracken, black in the moonlight. Sven eased beside her, and she felt an encouraging arm across her shoulders.

Catla searched for the pathway. How, by the hairy-tailed star, would they all manage to go down without rustling, tripping or falling? What had she been thinking?

Edith whispered against her ear. "You first, then Hugh, then Sven. I'll be last. Go slow."

Catla nodded but felt a little twitch of nervousness at the edge of her eye. At Edith's nudge, she entered the bracken, stretching out both hands to steady the fronds. Her fears welled again. The Nord-devils would hear her and they'd be waiting at the bottom to take her, because she was first, and put her—she shook her head, impatient with her fancies. She felt her way along, stooping, feet thrust forward. Had she been this slow before? She tried to move silently but the fronds' rattle sounded like an army of tinsmiths. Finally, she was through the bracken and into the alders. Almost halfway down, and on she went. Scudding clouds half hid the stars. The night seemed darker with leaves overhead. In younger days she'd imagined trees had fingers that would reach for her hair as she passed. With a great effort, she pushed that image away.

Twice she stopped to listen. The night stayed still. The rough texture of the boulder that marked the halfway point met her outstretched hands. Mossy patches covered some of the surface. Here the path curved to the left and widened. She moved faster, more confident now. Then she was on flat ground and in the oval glade, bounded by trees and bushes. She'd made it, and she felt a flutter of relief. A layer of ground fog drifted above the earth so it felt like she was wading through a cloud. The sky, brilliant with stars, gave her bits of light among the trees and bushes. On the far side, the bushes thinned, opening to the village.

She crossed and peered out, her heart bumping inside her ribs. There was the peat shed, her family just beyond it. She'd creep out for a look and be back before Hugh arrived. Only two steps later she heard a rustle and jumped back to the bottom of the path.

Hugh emerged. The clearing filled slowly with the dirty-faced villagers from Aigber. When Ragnar arrived, he was gagged and then tied to a tree. Edith came last.

"Now we begin." Hugh's whisper barely disturbed the air. He cupped his hands around his mouth and called the long low hunting hoot of an owl, hollow and eerie in the stillness. This first alert warned the group on Sven's path and the fishermen in the cove to prepare, to check their weapons and move into position. Everyone would wait for the wolf's howl before they moved closer. Hugh nodded. Catla stepped out of the clearing and glided across the foggy space to the peat shed. One by one, like silent, flitting phantoms, people gathered behind her.

The rank smell of peat caught the back of her nose, and she stifled a sneeze. The shed was more than half full. It hid them well as they crouched behind it. Catla peered around the corner in the predawn light and saw some people sitting up in the pen, but mostly she saw humps on the ground. The morning chorus of birdsong filled the air. She took it as an omen of luck.

Three Norsemen stood guard outside the pen. A small fire flickered. She held up three fingers to the rest of the group.

Hugh and the others crowded beside her to look.

Two guards stood with their hands propped on their ax hilts, their heads drooping onto their chests, dozing. One stood, his back to the fire, facing the path into the village. Their heads were bare of helmets and their swords were sheathed. As the firelight flickered on the curved ax blades, she clenched her fists to stop her hands from trembling and held very still.

Three villagers eased past her, catapults dangling from their hands. These herders of Aigber boasted they'd never lost a goat or a lamb to a wolf. Hugh thumped their backs softly as they passed like seawater over brown boulders, so liquid they seemed. They stopped, fitted rocks into the slings and gathered the cords. Round and around the slings whirred and released. The guard who was awake turned and started to shout. His voice was cut off as a rock found its mark. He and his comrades slumped to the ground with scarcely a sigh.

The rescuers rushed forward. Their feet rustled, but all else was quiet. Now, the prisoners who'd been sitting silently roused their sleeping neighbors. Outside the pen, one of the guards pushed himself up onto his hands and knees and then stood, blood running in a dark streak from his forehead. He raised his sword as he righted himself and held it unsteadily in front of him. Hugh's stave knocked the Norseman's arm aside and the sword clattered to the ground.

Hugh's words hissed in the darkness. "Remember, they're to be slaves. No one is to die. Everyone lives."

Sven's knife lunged, then stopped short of the guard's chest.

Catla's heart lurched.

The guard lifted his arms high into the air, then interlaced his fingers and placed them on top of his head. Hugh dragged the guard's hands down and tied them behind his back. Sven stuffed his mouth with soft batting. The other guards were gagged and bound like bundles of wool. The silence went undisturbed.

Catla watched the Covehithe prisoners as their eyes flashed in wonder and their fingers sealed their mouths.

They gestured frantically to each other to keep silent. Catla's mother placed her hand snugly across Bega's mouth. Cuthbert and Dunstan had sealed their mouths with their own hands. Catla was proud of their quick understanding. The people were silent, but their faces split with grins of joy and their hands waved in celebration and thanks.

Catla made eye contact with her mother and father and bounced up and down on her toes with impatience to free them. Her joy threatened to burst into a long shout, but she managed to stifle her cries. Hugh, struggling to loosen the knot holding the gate closed, took his knife and sliced it through. Catla pushed the gate open and reached for her mother and Bega. Her father's hand rested briefly on her head, Cuthbert's arms hugged her legs, and Dunstan squeezed her waist. The tight little pack shuffled to one side and then everyone squeezed out of the prison. She heard muffled laughter and the words, "No killing," muttered again and again. As quickly as the pen emptied, it was filled with the tightly trussed Norsemen.

Hugh whispered to Sarah and Brida to take the women and children to the clearing where they'd wait until the fighting was over. Catla walked with Sarah, Bega and her brothers. Her father caught her in his arms as she passed and then released her, whispering,

"Later, Catla. We'll talk later." He stood beside Hugh. Olav nodded to her briefly. Her heart stopped for a moment and she gaped at him. *No, I'll think about it eventually.* Brida wrinkled her nose and scowled; she'd come to fight, not sit with children. Hugh reached over, tweaked her arm and Catla's. "Come right back," he whispered. "They won't need you, but we will. We'll wait."

Catla led Cuthbert around the peat shed and into the clearing. It was a silent procession. Catla whispered the plans to Sarah, who said she'd fight too. Rebecca would take charge of the children and women. Catla's heart swelled and thumped at the prospect of walking into danger alongside her warrior mother.

When they rejoined the others, someone handed Brida and Sarah short swords. Everyone was armed, many holding Norse weapons. Catla tried to loosen the tension in her body by bouncing her knees.

Hugh raised his head and howled like a wolf— the last signal—and a snake of chill slithered down Catla's back. Her eyes met her mother's.

She was ready.

Almost immediately, answering howls echoed back.

Hugh raised his arm. Forward.

The sun had not yet traveled to the earth's brim, but dawn was near. The pink and purple sky lit her mother's face with a rosy glow, and the predawn chill wrapped around Catla's ankles. Higher in the sky, wisps of fog broke loose from the offshore fogbank, twisted and dissolved.

Catla swiveled her head as they advanced toward the council fire, passing her cottage. The thatch was burned over the doorway as far back as the ridge-pole. The little purple flowers were gone, and she felt a pang of sadness. Farther along, Martha's cottage was blackened, its roof completely burned away, the walls standing stark to the sky. The smell of smoke, acrid and nasty, caught the back of Catla's throat, and her sadness twisted into anger.

Several villagers left the group, searching inside and around each cottage. Muffled grunts and oaths erupted from inside one of the cottages and Sarah sped toward the doorway. A sword flew out and landed past her feet. She snatched it, turned and slashed, cutting the arm of a man in a black tunic fleeing from inside the cottage. Her sword immediately shifted to his chin and his shout was stifled as he stopped, eyes and mouth wide with shock.

Athelstan appeared at her side, clapping her on the back softly and whispering in her ear. She smiled a grim smile and nodded. He took a twist of leather from his pouch and batting from Sven, and in a twitch the man was on his way to the goat pen to join his comrades. Catla stood rooted, shocked at the suddenness of the action, until her mother took her elbow and urged her forward.

The sharp crack of wood breaking stopped her. Her foot lifted and hovered in midstep. She'd not seen the burnt stick on the path. The sound reverberated as her body turned to stone. Would the Norsemen hear that? Nothing moved. Her mother's hand edged her forward again. Then she saw them, the sleeping bodies of the Nord-devils. They were in the council circle between the cottages and the sea cliffs. They lay in a circle with their feet toward the central fire that had died to flickers and embers. There were only a few of them. Helgi's ship had not arrived.

Movement caught her eye and she glimpsed silent shapes gliding down from the hillside along Sven's path. The hill group came to a halt on the other side of the council ring to stop any Norsemen from escaping that way.

She looked across the fire and saw the fishermen stealing toward the sleeping Norsemen, carrying nets. The light increased as the morning sky glowed a pale blue. The pinks turned to rose, and details emerged. With soft air brushing her cheeks, the whole scene felt dreamlike.

One Norseman shook his head and stretched. To his right another scratched under his arm and rolled over to check for his sword. His wild hair stuck out at all angles. A knife blade gleamed, catching the fire's flickering coals. The invaders grunted and peered around, but there was no warning cry. Then three other men stretched and sat up.

Catla tightened her grip on her stave.

"For Covehithe!" Her mother's cry started the rush.

Shrieking, Catla joined her. A fishermen's net settled over the three men who were awake. They scrambled and tried to claw their way out of it, but the villagers tightened the net. Another net settled over two men still rousing from sleep and the third net whirled and trapped the last four who struggled to leap up, not yet fully awake.

"Grab them. Pull the nets hard now. Steady," yelled Matthew.

Catla's stave whacked the nearest man. His howl made her grimace.

Villagers pushed past her.

The Norsemen roared in frustration and pain as the nets closed around them and kicks and blows rained down on them. More Norse shouting came from behind the villagers at the bottom of Sven's path. Catla had expected all the Norsemen to be sleeping together in one place. The new furor horrified her. Immediately, she jumped on a seating log in the council ring for a better view. A different group of Norsemen appeared, brandishing their swords and shouting.

"They're coming from the oven shed and grain storage enclosure," Catla shouted and pointed.

The villagers at the bottom of Sven's path were taken by surprise, but they turned to face the enemy with swords raised.

A Norse voice shouted in English, "Die, you peasant dogs!" Voices roared as the group rushed toward the villagers. One swing of a Norse ax cut two Aigber men down. There was a crush of bodies as the Norsemen clashed against the villagers. Behind the villagers, the netted men had overbalanced and toppled out of the council ring, directly in front of the Aigber group. The villagers were caught between the two bands of invaders. The space they needed to wield their swords was limited. Many of them held short knives in their hands, but short knives were no match against war axes.

Athelstan had heard Catla's cry, and his teeth braced in a snarl. "Catla, to me." He yanked her beside him. "Stay here. They'll not take us that easily." He swept her around behind his back with one arm until she was half hidden.

With a leap, Sarah joined them, screaming an inarticulate war cry. A Norse ax lay in front of Athelstan, and he scooped up it up. He leaped forward as a Norseman swung his ax in a wild arc and another Aigber villager fell.

"Room, I need room." Athelstan picked up the net on the path and threw it and the two men in it across the council ring. They rolled close to the fire.

The villagers opened a way for Athelstan, who raised the ax over his right shoulder with both hands and swung, shouting a curse. A Norseman fell, blood spurting from a long gash across his chest. The blade also caught his companion, who dropped to the ground, screaming and twitching in agony.

"No killing, you ox." Hugh roared from behind Athelstan. "We need them all to sell."

"Hold fast," Athelstan shouted back. "I'm done. They needed to be taught a lesson. They took three of yours. Better their blood than more of ours."

Catla could hardly keep track; it had all happened so fast. But now she was shocked anew to hear these two old friends, these fast companions, yelling at each other. Had her father just killed two men? She looked at her mother, who was smiling broadly. "Back in battle, like the old days," she said and moved to take Athelstan's arm.

Catla shook her head, stunned by what she'd seen. She peered beyond her parents and saw other villagers disarming the rest of the Norsemen. They'd all backed away and raised their hands in surrender after their leader had fallen. Other villagers scouted the woods and fields to make sure none were hiding. Finally, all the invaders were captured and trussed.

Catla looked back to the council ring. The wounded men from Aigber lay there. Edith bent over them and was ripping lengths of cloth from her shift to bind wounds. Catla ran to her side. "Let me help, Edith. I'm Rebecca's apprentice. I can help."

"Good, Catla. I wish we were home. I suspect Rebecca's herbs and ointments have been burned. We'll do what we can. After the prisoners are secured, we'll get Rebecca from the grove and she'll help too."

The prisoners were released from the nets, disarmed and bound. These new prisoners were marched, with swords and short knives at their necks and backs, to join their companions in the council ring. Hugh and Athelstan moved after them.

Rufus arrived with Ragnar. The scowl on Ragnar's face deepened when the Norsemen jeered and shuffled past him. He looked at the men, sneered back at them and spat on the ground at their feet. He showed them no sympathy.

Sarah joined Edith and Catla to help bandage the villagers. Then she said to Catla, "You must be shocked, my daughter, to see the way of war."

Catla nodded. "Yes, yes, I am. When we left Aigber we were sure there would be no more killing, and now, all told, there are three dead Norsemen and three wounded men from Aigber. I know war kills people, but seeing it makes me feel sick."

"That is exactly the right reaction. Killing is never a good thing. Your father and I have killed in order to save our land and the lives of our own. We'll talk about this later, but now we need some chamomile tea to settle you."

Catla agreed. Then Sarah pointed to Ragnar. "Who is that?"

"That's Ragnar, Mother. He's a Norseman. It's odd, but I think he's a good one. I met him crossing the heath on the way back."

"Really, Catla? We have many things to talk about. My dreamy daughter who lives in the clouds has indeed landed on earth!" She snorted when Catla rolled her eyes.

Quickly, the council ring filled with happy laughter and the joyous high-pitched voices of the women and children from the grove. Rebecca hurried to Sarah,

Edith and Catla to examine the wounded villagers from Aigber.

"You've done well here. These men will need looking after, but their wounds are clean."

Catla said, "There are Norse prisoners who need tending to as well, Rebecca."

"You're learning the healer's role," said Rebecca. "This is part of healing, to tend any who need help."

Catla went with her to the two men who had stopped moving. Blood pooled on the ground beside them. Rebecca placed her finger on each throat to feel for any life force. She shook her head. "The wounds were deep. They have left this world, but they died fighting, so a place in the warrior heavens will be theirs. We will prepare them for the ground."

As Rebecca was speaking, Hugh raised his arms in the air. Victory! He grabbed Athelstan's hand, and Catla felt a surge of love and pride for her father. A mighty cheer split the sky, and the heavenly witness, the pole star, though fading, jiggled in front of Catla's eyes.

CHAPTER FIFTEEN

home

Sarah whirled Catla around in a lively jig.

"Let's dance and sing. Put the gloom and fear away. Let's be happy and celebrate, my warrior daughter," Sarah said, blinking the tears away. "I'm so proud of you."

"You are? Thank you. I am proud of you too, Warrior Mother."

"Oh." Sarah laughed. "I'm not really a warrior any more, although the fight did stir my blood this day. You need to learn how to handle the short sword. That lesson is long overdue."

"But, Mother, I'm a healer's apprentice." Catla wasn't sure she wanted to be a warrior.

"Nonsense, Catla. You should see Rebecca handle a sword. She does it well. It's a necessary tool for life." Then she broke off and held Catla at arm's length. "Everyone in the village is so grateful to you. I am too. Grateful and proud. You and the people of Aigber have saved our village."

"But anyone would have done what I did, and don't forget Sven."

"No, no, my child. It was you. You saw the savagery and still acted. That's what matters. You did it! And I am going to have to stop calling you *my child*, for you have truly passed into womanhood."

Conflicting emotions flooded Catla's mind. "Won't I always be your child?" she asked. Was she a woman now? She didn't feel different. Part of her hoped things could remain the same, but too much had happened in the last two days. Her mother was right: she had changed. Suddenly she knew she could not marry Olav. She didn't know how she would do it, but she knew she had to break the betrothal. But what about her vow? What about that? There were things to sort out, that much was clear. Olav was one. Helgi was another.

"Look at Father." Catla spied Athelstan across the council circle standing a little apart, shoulders slumped and face weary. "Let's cheer him up."

She grabbed her mother's hand, and they ran and leaped into his arms. He staggered under their weight but laughed. "You two great bears. Get off before my back breaks." Under his gruff words Catla heard the same joy and relief she felt coursing through her body. "Catla. We prayed you were all right. We were afraid for you, afraid you might have been captured too."

"I was afraid for me too." She laughed and hugged her father back. "But I was more frightened for you, every moment until the pen was opened and I saw you. Are Bega and Cuthbert and—"

"Nay, child. No worries. We are hungry and still shocked, but unharmed," Athelstan said.

"The men didn't touch us women," Sarah continued. Then a twinkle came to her eye and she added, "I'm not sure why. Perhaps the smell of goats was not to their liking."

Now Catla's tears swelled down her cheeks in relief.

"I want to hear it all," her mother said. "You got help in Aigber. Where did you meet Sven? I sensed you were safe even as I was afraid to hope. We have much to tell each other."

Talk, laughter and more greetings mingled in the fresh morning light as people from both villages greeted each other in thanksgiving.

"We did it."

"We beat the Norse bullies!"

"Let's hear it for the people of Aigber."

Catla joined in the cheers and laughter. She felt content. The sun's rays broke through the fog bank, and the sunrise colors paled and dissipated. The slanting light lit people's faces, most of them grimy from the dirt used to blend into the dark night, others filthy from goat droppings. They pointed and laughed at each other, then washed using water collected from the rivulet on the far side of the cove. Other folks jumped right into a small pool in the stream created years before for that very purpose.

The devastation of the village showed plainly now in the new light: small cottages with burnt thatch, blackened and half-burnt walls. The Covehithe women went to their hearths and started their fires from the council fire embers, gathered what little food they could find and prepared it for the pots. In the midst of the destruction, people still needed to be fed. Catla hadn't looked closely at her small cottage when she'd passed it in the dim morning light except to see the burnt thatch and missing flowers. Now she wanted to inspect it carefully. Black soot framed the opening and covered part of the outside walls. She swallowed past a lump in her throat and went in. All the sleeping robes were there, scorched and covered with ashes. Catla lifted her robes and checked for her knife and golden coin. The knife was there. The coin was missing. *Spoils of war.* She felt a pang of regret but shrugged and took the robes outside, wrinkling her nose at their odor. The fur had been burned away in a few places where thatch had fallen, so the hide showed, blackened and brittle.

She raised her eyes to the walls, dark from the smoke of years of cooking over the central hearth fire. Toward the roofline they were even darker. The small clay lamp was missing from its niche. The tanned goat hide, used as a summer door cover, had been torn off, crumpled in a heap and kicked aside.

"Heathen devils," Catla said. Even so, she felt relief. Her home was standing, and everything could be fixed.

"I expected worse," Sarah said beside her. "Did you give the robes a good shake?"

At Catla's nod, she continued, "Then look to see if there's anything in the kitchen garden we can put in the pottage. The broth will be thin if we can't find enough vegetables to thicken it and give it some flavor. We'll need oats too."

In the small garden the herbs and vegetables were trampled. "Nord-devils," Catla muttered aloud in anger, pulling at shoots of garlic greens mashed into the dirt.

Catla and Sarah worked, adding to the pottage. Then Hugh called Catla's name. Catla looked down the pathway that led from her home, through the grove of aspens and alders, to the council ring. He waved at her. She waved back. He beckoned her and called, "Catla, come here."

She waved again to show she'd heard.

Her mother said, "Go. This is part of your story now. We have days and days to talk."

As Catla started to walk, a warm little hand grasped hers and she looked down.

Bega smiled up at her. "Catla, where were you?"

"Oh, Bega, come with me." Holding hands, they walked toward Hugh. Folks smiled at her and moved aside so a narrow path opened before them all the way to the council ring. Catla felt pats on her back and arms as she moved. Sven was already standing beside Hugh, and as Hugh's hand beckoned her forward, her face started to burn. She gulped and squeezed Bega's hand. She hated fuss. Of any kind.

"You sad, Catla?" Bega asked.

"No. I am not sad, but I'm not happy. Everyone's looking at me."

"Be happy. I hold your hand."

Catla smiled at her little sister's wisdom and felt the muscles in her face relax slightly. Pulling Bega close to her side, she stepped up beside Hugh and Sven. When she looked out at the faces of her friends, she couldn't help but smile. Edith caught her eye. Now her smile broke into a genuine beam of joy.

Hugh engulfed Catla and Sven in a huge hug, one to each arm. When people hushed their talk, he said, "These two quick-thinking, brave young people have saved our villages. We're here to celebrate because of them. Their warning came in time for us to capture the Norsemen in Aigber. They knew by helping us, Covehithe would get help. Together we won against brute strength. Today we are not slaves. We are free. Thank you, Catla and Sven." He gripped her left wrist and Sven's right one and lifted their arms high.

A mighty whoop rose into the morning air. Pleased but still embarrassed by the many eyes on her, Catla smiled back at her friends. A feeling of contentment and thanksgiving settled inside her. The Covehithe dogs ran around and got in everyone's way. Catla saw Stoutheart. Her heart thudded. He was safe! She'd been so afraid he'd been killed. "Stoutheart," she called and as soon as he saw her, he waved his plumed tail and trotted over, grinning, his tongue hanging over the side of his mouth. He stuck his nose into her open hand, and she knelt with Bega as they both threw their arms around his neck. People clapped, hugged their neighbors and patted each other's backs.

Hugh raised his arm for silence once more. "Before we get too far into our celebration, let us remind ourselves we have things to discuss at council. Helgi will arrive with a crew of warriors, today or on the morrow, by our reckoning. You don't know Ragnar, our Norse friend, but he will tell us what he knows. Athelstan, will you call a council?"

Athelstan nodded. Hugh held up his hand and said, "Come to Athelstan's council at the wolf's call. We'll find our answers. Talk to each other. What can we do to foil Helgi? Soon we will have our food and ale."

Catla made slow progress, winding her way to her cottage through the crowd as people thanked her with hugs and pats on the back. The council circle emptied as cottages were inspected. Debris was being cleared from hearths and fires had been lit. Pots filled with water to cook the short-shadow meal hung on the metal supports.

Women's voices called back and forth as they explored their cottages and shared what they needed. The women from Aigber helped, and soon the cottages hummed like a honey tree full of bees.

As Catla handed garlic, onions and a cabbage to her mother, she remembered her unpleasant decision. "Mother, where's Olav? I thought he'd be anxious to see me."

Sarah avoided her eyes as she handed Catla some cut up cabbage for the pot. "There's been a change."

"Is he hurt? He seemed fine when I saw him outside the goat pen."

"No, but—"

"I'm sorry, Mother," Catla interrupted. "I don't mean to be rude, but I cannot marry him. I thought I could, and I even made a vow that I would go through with the betrothal if you were all safe when I returned home. But, Mother, I can't. I just can't."

"Father John thinks Olav would be kind to you, Catla. You'll grow to like him. Our lord has agreed to the match."

"Would you have married someone you didn't like, Mother?"

Sarah was silent for a moment before she said, "So that's how things are. Is there nothing about him you find attractive?"

"No. I really don't like him at all."

"Your father will be upset."

"I'll talk to him as soon as I have the chance." Catla squared her shoulders and turned her back on Sarah.

"Well, there is something that may influence things. I was just going to tell you. During our time in the pen, Martha was hysterical."

Catla turned back to face her mother.

"Olav was the only one who could calm her. She clung to him. It was disgraceful."

I can see her doing it, Catla thought. *She always cries for what she wants.* "Didn't Father tell Martha that Olav had spoken for me?" Catla was surprised at her indignation. It was all so confusing. She didn't want Olav, but she didn't want him to be with someone else. It made no sense.

"She knew. We didn't say anything. Everything was so uncertain. No one knew what would happen to us all. And it seemed to solve everyone's problems. And now you tell me you don't want him after all."

"I don't, but what about Olav? Won't he feel obligated to complete his betrothal promise? Aren't people talking about this?"

"Yes, now that you're home, Olav will consider himself betrothed to you. He will say he was comforting Martha as a friend, but he'll still expect to marry you." Sarah and Catla continued cutting up vegetables as they paused to think.

"Well, now I feel pushed aside like some...some spoiled onion," Catla said. "What kind of a man is he? Do you think he'll be anxious to be rid of the betrothal? Martha already knows how to behave like a wife. Maybe he'd rather have her. They are closer in age."

"Ah, you are definitely a woman now, Catla. We don't like to be passed over. We want to be the ones to decide our own fates. And I see your point about Olav. We'll see what your father has to say. He has to be considered as well. I don't know the way Olav thinks."

"Father's not the one who will have to live with Olav in York…" Her voice died as she looked at the frown on her mother's face. She knew her mother was right. She grew quiet. The talk with Mother had gone better than she had anticipated. Father had to be considered. She wondered if there was some way out of this mess with everyone getting what they wanted, and no one appearing to have lost anything important.

"I hope Martha feels guilty," Catla said. "Stealing a betrothed man. I'd like to see them both squirm." Even as she said it, she realized it wasn't true. She wanted to be free of Olav, and Martha was doing her a favor.

"Nay, Catla. Your kindness is stronger than your pique. We have to live with them, remember. Besides, if you act in a nasty way, Martha will feel justified and righteous in saving Olav from you, not uncomfortable. She'll be able to say she saved him from a shrew." Sarah grinned at her daughter.

A wail arose from Martha's place, two cottages away. Catla raised her eyebrows. "There she goes again. Shall we see what it's about this time?"

Mother and daughter found Martha sobbing. "I can't live here. Look at it." The front wall was in one piece, but the top half of the back and south walls were burned away. Everything was blackened and burned. The thatch was gone from all but the northwest corner of the roof. Charred timbers and clods of thatch lay on top of the sleeping robes and pots on the hard-packed earthen floor.

"Oh, Martha," said Sarah. "Those horrible men!"

Catla watched her mother pat Martha's back and realized that the scene was familiar. She'd witnessed Martha's wailing all her life.

Olav, you'll be getting more than you bargained for.

As if she had called him with her mind, Olav appeared in the doorway of the cottage, then stopped abruptly when he saw Catla and Sarah with Martha.

"Hello, Olav," Catla's voice was cool. "Martha is upset about the state of her cottage. Are you well?"

He gulped but he hurried forward and clasped her hands. "Very well, thank you. Catla, you have done a wonderful thing for these two villages." Then he paused and gulped again, but Catla spoke before he could continue.

"I need to talk to you, Olav. But now is not the time or the place. We'll get Martha settled and then I'll come and find you. We'll walk down to the grove and back. Is that all right with you?" Catla kept her face clear of expression.

"That is…I want to talk to you as well. That is…" He sputtered to a halt.

"Fine then. I'll be along soon. Martha is calming down."

After they got Martha settled, Catla took a deep breath for courage and stepped onto the path toward her home. Once there, she gave the pottage a few more stirs and glanced at Olav lingering outside the door. Catla stepped out to join him, smiled and said, "Shall we walk down toward the grove? We'll cut through the trees and avoid the goat pen."

Olav nodded in agreement and moved to take her arm, but Catla sidestepped his hand, turned and walked beside him. She said, "Mother tells me that you helped Martha when you were all imprisoned in the goat pen."

Olav's hard gaze lingered on her face as he said, "Yes. The poor woman was in great distress. It seemed to everyone there that I was most able to calm her and restore some peace. The guards were threatening to gag her if she couldn't be quiet, and that terrified both her and her sons."

"I can see that would have been nasty. But tell me, Olav, have you found feelings for Martha?"

"Well," he sputtered, and his face turned a dull red, "she appreciates me, which is more than you have ever done."

Catla sighed as she thought, *This is going to be tedious*, but she nodded and said, "Perhaps you'd rather be with Martha. I am willing to release you from your promised betrothal if we can arrange an agreement."

"Agreement?" The scowl lifted from Olav's face. "What kind of an agreement?"

"Both of us need to maintain our reputations in this village. It is my home, and my father is headman. He cannot appear to have a foolish daughter. Soon it may be your home too."

"My dear child, I have never thought of you as foolish. Perhaps you are dreamy and carefree, but not foolish. What are you suggesting?"

Catla grated her teeth at his choice of words. She was certainly not his dear child.

"I will say I approve of your choice of Martha for a wife, if you tell everyone that because I have a gentle and kind spirit, I have allowed you to choose Martha and will make no demands over the broken betrothal. And in return you are gifting me with a length of cloth, large enough to make a new apron."

This last part had just occurred to her as she spoke, and she held very still to see what he would think of it. Her heart pounded as he kept his silence. Catla could not imagine what he was thinking. Her mind was racing as it skirted over many possibilities: that he would tell her father that his daughter was demanding payment to get out of an honorable agreement, or that he would decide he wanted her after all, or that he didn't want either of them and he'd tell everyone that Catla was a little schemer. None of these possibilities would suit her. She dug her fingers into the palms of her hands while she waited, holding the inside of her cheek with her teeth to prevent herself from speaking first.

Finally, Olav stopped walking and faced her, but still he did not speak. After a moment she lowered her eyes so as not to betray her nervousness. Then he finally spoke. "You are a clever girl, Catla. I think I have underestimated you. But I also think you have come up with a way that will please us both. We will all maintain our dignity here in Covehithe. I agree to your plan. And just so you know, I had already purchased a length of cloth, enough for a robe. It's from Italia, so you know I have chosen it for you carefully."

"Oh, Olav, perhaps it is I who has underestimated you. But I thank you." She put out her right hand, and he solemnly took it and raised it to his lips.

"I think we should both tell my parents, don't you?"

Back in her own cottage, after Olav had left, her father and mother looked at her and smiled, their pride showing in their eyes.

Catla hugged herself and said, "I feel lighter than goose down right now. I was so worried about everything—the Norsemen, Olav, all of you, me."

"Nay, Catla, you did well." Athelstan was clearly relieved. "That is the happiest breakup of a betrothal I have ever seen. He and Martha will do nicely together."

As Catla scoured some fresh parsnips for the food pot, she realized that she bore Olav and Martha no ill will. Her father was right: they were well suited.

A great cheer went up outside. Elene had found some ale.

Catla foraged in the gardens again and found more onions, a few more parsnips, turnips and another cabbage. Her heart lightened as she tugged them out of the earth, dusted off the dirt and took them inside for the pot. Food was cooking, and it smelled of the dried herbs her mother had added. Her hollow stomach rumbled as she cut the vegetables into small pieces so they would cook quickly.

"I've not found any ale," Elene's neighbor, Chelsea, called out. "Has anyone, besides Elene, found any?"

The Norsemen might have drunk all they could find, but Catla knew her village. There would be more than one barrel cached away someplace.

"Mother, did you check the root cellar? I'll do it, if you like." She put her arm around her mother's waist, gave it a squeeze, and said, "I'm going to help more. And I've eaten more than you have in the last two days." At her mother's arched eyebrows, Catla thought, *Just you wait and see. I'm different now.*

"Yes, check the root cellar. See if there are more oats too."

Chelsea called out again. "I've found a piece of ham. It was curing under the eaves and it's still there. The Norsemen missed it in the gloom. I'll cut a chunk for each pot. That'll improve the taste of things."

Catla collected the meat from Chelsea and watched her mother cut it up and add it to the pot.

Sven approached with a determined stride and called to her. "Catla, I've had an idea. I'd like to talk about it."

Sarah said, "There's Sven. You two have much to talk about. Your father is there with the others. Go join them."

Catla gave her mother a quick hug and slipped out to meet Sven, who said, "Your brothers and Martha's sons want to use Martha's cottage as their new holding pen. It's not fit for any other kind of shelter. So I've given our cottage—father's and mine—to Martha and her sons. Most of the roof is still there, so it will give some shelter. Father was already talking about moving to Chester. He won't want to live here again, I don't think."

"You mean *Olav* and Martha and her sons."

"Olav? I thought he and you..."

Catla shook her head.

"It's over?" Sven asked.

Catla nodded.

"Do you mind?"

"Not at all. I never wanted to marry him, but I wanted to please everyone: my parents, our lord and Father John. Olav's giving me a piece of cloth from Italia, enough to make a robe, as a token of his respect." She smiled. What was it about Sven that made it so easy for her to talk to him?

He stepped closer. "I'll need a place to stay. I'd like sleep in your cottage, now that Martha and Olav will have mine. Of course, I'll have to stay on the far side of the hearth from your sleeping robes."

"Yes, with Cuthbert and Dunstan." Catla smiled at the thought of their thrashing legs and elbows bumping into Sven all night. "I'm not sure how you'll like it."

"Let me decide. I think it will suit me."

"It might suit you, but I think Father will have much to say about it. You'd be better to ask Rebecca."

"Oh. I was hoping you'd ask your father for me."

"No. It is kind of you to let Martha and Olav have your place. They'll be much more comfortable, but I can't ask if you can stay with us. I'm sorry."

Sven reached for Catla's hand and held it for moment. Catla felt a little thrill of pleasure. Sven was a close friend now, after all their shared experiences, and she was happy to have him hold her hand. But she couldn't imagine him sleeping in her cottage.

The sky was blue and cloudless. The sun had moved well past short-shadow time. Catla sighed with contentment. The food was cooking. Her mother had shooed her out to meet Sven. Most of the dread of the past two days lifted. Then she frowned. Helgi. Were they talking about Helgi? How could he and his men be outwitted? There was no time to make a trap. Something about their black tunics nudged her mind, but an idea would not form. Other people would be planning strategies to use against him too. Her family, the whole village and the people of Aigber, whom she had come to know so well, were all still in danger of being captured, hurt or killed. What could they do against Helgi? A cloud appeared and passed over the sun. The day grayed. "Why the frown?" Sven asked.

Catla looked at him and her frown eased. "I keep thinking about Helgi. Aren't you worried?"

"We'll be ready for Helgi when he comes."

Catla thought his reply was light and too hasty, but she had seen how ingenious the villagers were and a sudden surge of faith filled her. Something would occur to someone. As the cloud shifted past the sun, a small hand crept into hers. She looked down at Bega, who said, "Catla, I have something. I kept it for you when we were in the goat pen."

"What is it, Bega?"

The small hand opened and Catla saw the round golden coin she had thought was lost. Not a spoil of war after all.

"Oh, Bega. Lovely! Thank you. What a clever girl you are. It's my lucky coin!" She slipped it into the pouch hanging from her belt.

Catla knelt to hug her small sister, and they both giggled in delight. When she stood, she reached for Bega's hand again and then placed her other hand in Sven's. Together they walked to join her father, her lucky coin jostling in the pouch against her side. The sun warmed her back and she felt comforted. Her family and friends were safe. Everyone was ready for a celebration and some food and drink. She grinned suddenly as she dropped Sven's hand, scooped up Bega and called, "Race you," over her shoulder. And as she sped to join her father and the other villagers, her heart lifted and she felt as if she could run forever.

Author's Note

The history of the Vikings is fascinating and complicated. Vikings came from the Scandinavian countries of Norway, Sweden and Denmark. They traveled to and settled in many parts of the world from Russia to North America. The first Viking attack in England was in 793 AD and history accepts that by the end of 1066, the Viking Age in England was essentially over.

Swedish Vikings settled farther east in Russia. Viking Danes and Norsemen settled in England, Scotland, Ireland, Greenland, Iceland, Normandy and Sicily. In England, they became merchants, craftsmen and farmers, but there were still those who waged war and raided for trade goods, gold and slaves. Vikings traveled widely over the known world and created trade routes. Warrior Vikings were greatly feared and frequently were paid vast sums of money to leave places in peace.

In 1066, there was a rebellion close to York, in Northumbria, not too far from Catla's village. The previous year, northern lords had ousted Tostig, brother to the King of England, from his position as Earl of Northumbria. In his anger, Tostig conspired against his brother by inviting the King of Norway to invade England and claim England's throne. The Norse king had already created trouble by proclaiming he was the legitimate heir to the throne.

That autumn, hundreds of Norse ships crossed the North Sea. Some of them sailed up the River Humber to York, where three great battles were fought. The invaders won the first two, but the English king won the third one, at Stamford Bridge, just outside of the city of York.

Catla's world had been settled and prosperous for the past few decades before her story begins a few days after the battle at Stamford Bridge. I've recreated the social setting as closely as possible, but Catla, the villagers, the locations of the villages, the circle of standing stones and the hill fort are all fiction. Nevertheless, I have strived for historical accuracy as much as possible. For example, Halley's Comet did appear in April of 1066 and was recorded worldwide. People called it the hairy-tailed star and considered it an omen.

Village people traveled by cart or walked with a pack, as did Olav the peddler. Some footpaths were worn so deeply into the ground they are still visible today. Peddlers were the early merchants. They walked many miles and traded or bought goods with coins. In the villages, most trade was bartered.

Only the wealthy kept horses. Oxen pulled the plows. Sheep and goats were milked and village people grew their food, fished and hunted. Captured people were sold at slave markets in Ireland, Paris and other places. While slavery was in common practice worldwide, not everyone kept slaves.

Although Catla's world was very different from ours, some things never change: greed, envy, thirst for power, compassion, love and truth. Catla's desire to find her own way in the world is a desire we all share.

Acknowledgments

This book would not have been written without these words of encouragement from my family: "Go for it, Mum." Thank you, Gordon, Craig, Dan and Laura. My granddaughter, Clara, was my first young reader, and I thank her for her quick eye and hearty endorsement. Friends and extended family have also encouraged me and I am grateful. Writing groups both in Victoria and in Calgary contributed invaluable research, comments, enthusiasm and interest over the story's long gestation. The Banff Centre for the Arts gave me space to write, as did Yellow Point Lodge. Thanks go also to the helpful people in the museums in York and Rye, for filling in some of the gaps. Betty Jane Hegerat provided me with close reads, sensitive feedback and constant encouragement, and I thank her. And lastly, thanks to the folks at Orca Book Publishers who thought Catla should have her story told, and to editor, Sarah Harvey, for seeing me through the process.

Born in Calgary, Mary Elizabeth Nelson has been both a teacher-librarian and a language arts teacher. She wrote her first book at age four. Her interest in all things medieval started with fairy tales and books such as the *Count of Monte Cristo*. Mary's textbook *Medieval Times* (*L'époque médiévale*) is used in Ontario schools. She has four children and three grandchildren and presently lives and writes on Vancouver Island, British Columbia.